RETURN TO
SOUTH TOWN

RETURN TO SOUTH TOWN

by Lorenz Graham

12037

Thomas Y. Crowell Company
New York

Manufactured in the United States of America

Library of Congress Cataloging in Publication Data
Graham, Lorenz B
  Return to South Town.
  SUMMARY: In spite of the difficulties it might bring, David Williams, now a full-fledged doctor, returns to establish his practice in the Virginia town where he had lived as a boy.
  [1. Afro-Americans—Fiction. 2. Race problems—Fiction] I. Title.
PZ7.G7527Re   [Fic]   75-33712
ISBN 0-690-01081-8

1 2 3 4 5 6 7 8 9 10

To my wife, Ruth,
constant companion and helpful critic

With thanks to Dr. James H. Bowles
and to Dr. Herbert E. Johnson
for their help in telling this story

One

As he drove south everything he saw was new. Nothing seemed to be as he remembered it. The cities seemed shiny new with high-reaching buildings gleaming with stainless steel and glass. Domed auditoriums loomed on the skyline and bright-colored motor inns beckoned to him. Cars and trucks moved swiftly with the speeding traffic on the wide expressways.

He was not driving in the fast lane. There was plenty of time. He moved the Volkswagen steadily without trying to pass others who were driving faster than the speed limit. He wanted to see and feel the changes all about him.

Surely it was different from when he had lived in the South.

"But I guess I'm different too," he said, speaking aloud to himself. Then he thought, not speaking the words, "I'm different, older, but not so old that I have to talk to myself."

He had read that the old Jim Crow laws had been set aside. Sit-ins, marches, riots, and all kinds of revolutionary struggles had led to court decisions which protected for him and all other blacks the rights of full citizenship. People had told him that changes had been made, that he would be able to eat in all the restaurants and stop in any of the hotels or motels throughout the South.

He drove through Capital City, but by the time he reached Clarksburg he was hungry. Out of the many advertised eating places he selected a high rising motor hotel and turned right to leave the express highway.

"If I'm going to have trouble," he told himself, "it might as well be in a decent place."

In the parking lot he found a vacant slot. He drew his long frame out of the VW and gave a sigh of relief as he straightened to his full height.

A wide glass door opened before him automatically at his approach. Inside a smiling hostess greeted him.

"Just one?" she asked as she turned to lead him down the aisle.

People were looking at him but he was used to that. More than six feet tall, with wide shoulders, he looked like an athlete. He was dark in color. His features were heavy. People had mistaken him for one or another famous black professional football player. When they asked for his autograph he always responded, writing his "David Williams" with such a scrawl that it could not be read. And he would smile and move on.

In the North he felt that he knew what to expect. Here he was less at ease. He wished he were not alone. Someone might have shared his experience and helped him interpret the situation, the looks that people gave him, some with smiles and some with calm indifference.

At a table he held the menu before him as a waitress stood by with poised pencil. He ordered the lunch steak special with clam chowder, French fries, and coffee.

"How do you want your steak, sir?"

"Rare, I guess, maybe medium rare."

As the girl picked up the menu and walked away he looked around. No one now was looking at him. No one seemed surprised to see a black man ordering lunch. Then across the room he saw a whole family of black people, three children and their parents. Nobody was staring at them either.

It gave him a good feeling. He was not alone.

The lunch was all right but he still wanted to talk about his feelings. When he got back on the highway he thought of picking up a hitchhiker. This four-lane one-way strip with landscaped banks on each side was new. It was one of the significant differences. He knew he was within a couple of hours' drive to South Town.

The map showed that old Route One paralleled the new road he was traveling.

At the next exit he left the new highway. A good paved road led off to the west. Where it crossed Route One, he turned left through the intersection toward the area in which he had been born thirty years earlier and where he had spent half of his life.

Now he saw hitchhikers.

One held up a card with an arrow. It read "Miami." Another was wearing an army blouse with sergeant's stripes on the sleeve. A large German police dog poised beside him in the position of heel.

"Not you or you," he said as he shook his head.

He had no thought of danger from those who might want to ride. He liked people. Usually when he was driving alone he picked up riders. He liked to hear what they had to say. Their stories were good for laughs and they supplied entertainment along the miles.

This day he wanted something more.

He wanted information about the country. He wanted to know how people were feeling. Without asking for it he wanted support for his plan to return to South Town.

As the car rolled toward the next intersection he saw another boy who seemed to want a ride. He was alone, a raw-boned country boy with red hair. He had books bound together with a strap. The boy ran forward as the car rolled to a stop and he gave hearty thanks as he got in and took his seat.

"How far you going?" David asked.

"To the community college," came the quick answer. "You know where it is?"

David said he did not know about the community college.

"It's just a couple miles from here. I live back up towards Alberta, about four miles. Mostly I drive, but my mother had to use the car today. I got a ride from my house to the highway. Started early, so I'm still on time for my first class. That is, if you're going that far."

"Oh, yes. I'm going on through into Pocahontas County. But this community college: How long has it been there?"

"Well, about three years, but it's still pretty new, like there wasn't anything there before. It's just about like high school, almost free for those that live in the district. Folks used to have to go away if they wanted to go to college, and that cost a lot."

"Yes. I remember."

"You from round here? I see you got license plates from up north."

"Yep. I'm from around here. Born near South Town. Been away a long time."

"Golly! I guess things have changed. You'll see it. I can remember how it was before, all the schools separate like for white and black, you know. That must have been the way it was when you went to school."

"Yep, that's the way it was. I was in tenth grade at Pocahontas County Training School when my folks moved away—mainly, I guess, to get better schooling for me."

"I bet you did find a better high school. Did you ever go to college?"

"Yes, I went to college."

"I guess if I'd have been away to college I wouldn't want to come back here. Oh . . . maybe just to see how things were."

"Then again, maybe you'd want to come back and settle down."

"In the South and in the country? Not me."

"But the South looks a lot better than it did when we moved away. Fine highways. Lots of brick houses. Electricity everywhere. And now a community college. A man might make a life here—and do some good."

"Well, maybe it's like my sociology prof says. She says this is a new South. She talks a lot about the way it used to be. I never thought much about it when I was little but it must have been right weird."

"Yes. I guess that's right." Neither spoke while the VW maneuvered its way around a double trailer truck, but David was remembering. When they were in the clear he turned to his passenger and said, "You're right. It was weird."

"So now you've been away, up north—in the cities, I guess." David was agreeing, and the boy went on, "So now are you thinking about coming back, back to this country scene? How come?"

"Maybe I like it in the country. Maybe I like the South?"

"Are you a farmer? Is that what you studied in college?"

"Not really. I studied medicine. Ever since I left here fifteen years ago I've been thinking about coming back, I've been wanting to return to South Town. I'll soon finish two years of specialty training. I'll be ready then to set up practice."

"Well, I bet you won't like it." The boy was shaking his head in disbelief. "You'll probably check out the town and the country round about and hightail it back up north and settle in some city. That's where the money is. But I get down at the next crossroad. That is, unless you want to turn off and take a look at the community college. I bet my sociology prof would like to meet you. She's a black woman."

He did not turn off.

Road signs marked the approach to South Town. David Williams recognized the familiar rolling country. The highway clung like a wide ribbon on the dips and rises. Patches of red clay lay on the gray concrete in streaks.

It was a warm spring day, two weeks before Easter. Most of the land had been plowed. On both sides of the highway sections were laid out in even furrows conforming to the contours of the land. It was tobacco country. Seed beds covered with shiny plastic glistened in the sun. Farmers were well into the season.

David remembered the long downhill stretch of the highway and a store which used to have a gasoline pump. Now the store was abandoned and falling into disrepair. On a concrete platform the last of the pump was twisted in somber rust.

Over the next rise he came suddenly to a new Holiday Inn with wide-swept lawns and parking for more than a hundred cars. Next to it a deluxe service station would surely have made the little gas pump at the crossroad store obsolete. Beyond that was a shopping center with a supermarket, a laundromat, a drugstore, a Woolworth five-and-dime, and other shops for sales and service.

Yes, South Town was different.

Two

He remembered it as a sleepy town with slow-moving people, and ladies sitting in rocking chairs on their front porches. In the neighborhood through which he drove most of the old frame houses had been replaced with brick buildings, and apartment houses rose among them.

At the traffic light he made the left turn to go down Main Street. Folsom's hardware store was still there, but one whole block had been reconstructed as a shopping center. At the end of the street was the Ford agency, just where he remembered it, but the building was new. That was where he had worked the last summer in South Town. Mr. Boyd, the owner, was the man who had made all the trouble for his family. South Town National Bank was across the street. Mr. Boyd had owned that too.

Old Route One made a right turn around the Ford agency. It ran south past the school David and his sister had attended, and went on toward the house where the Williams family had lived, about four miles from the town. The place was not a farm. It had less than five acres, but the family had kept a cow, a few hogs, and some chickens. David and his sister, Betty Jane, had shared in the work. Their father, Ed Williams, had worked in town as a mechanic. They had had electricity but few other modern conveniences. Everybody used the little house at the back.

When they moved away, Israel Crawford, a one-armed veteran of World War II who was a close friend, had bought the property. He was still living there with his family.

Some weeks before he left New York, David wrote the Crawfords to say that he was planning a visit.

"Come right on," Velvet, Israel's wife, had written in reply. "We sure be glad to see you."

He drove by a restaurant called the Pancake House. It advertised real southern fried chicken. An agency for farm implements displayed bright yellow and red tractors and trailers and accessories. He hardly recognized the hill on which the Pocahontas County Training School had stood. There was no school there. Three or four brick residences occupied the site.

The Crawfords' welcome was hearty. As David drove into the yard Israel came running from the back lot, shouting his greeting. Velvet came from the front door, crossing the porch and running down the steps.

She had her arms around David almost before he stepped from the car. A shaggy black dog barked his excitement.

With his one hand Israel pounded David on the back.

"Where you been so long?" he demanded. "I thought you done forgot all about your old friends. Great day in the morning. Sure is good to see you, boy."

"No boy now," Velvet put in. "He a full-growed man . . . bigger than you, Israel."

"Well, come on in the house. We got a lot of catching up to do. How's your mamma and your sister? What you been doing for yourself? How long can you stay with us?"

The questions came without pausing for answers.

Inside the house they showed the improvements, an extension for a bathroom at the back and a service porch with laundry equipment. Israel, Jr., was fifteen. He had David's old room.

There were four children. The three younger children were girls. They were all at school.

"You be sleeping in the girls' room, David," Velvet said. "We thought first we put you in your old room, but Junior, he want to stay around you much as he can."

"We figure that be good for the boy," Israel said.

"The girls be staying over to their Big Mamma's

much as we let them," Velvet said. "When they here I make them do some work. Big Mamma spoils them."

"Big Mamma" was Israel's mother. His father was dead. Israel spent most of his time at her place doing the farm work on the forty acres.

It was early afternoon. Although David said he was not hungry, Velvet made coffee and they sat at the table in the kitchen. The rush of unanswered questions was over. They were ready to talk calmly and to listen. For David Williams, absent for the past fifteen years, it was like making a report.

"Yes," he said, "Pa died nearly four years ago. Kind of worked himself to death, I guess. It was rough for him. He worked hard. Wanted me to stay in school. It took a lot out of him. He said it was worth it. But my mother is well. Maybe she'll be coming back here to live . . . with me. And my sister, she's teaching school and she talks about getting married. But Mom wants to come back here."

"You mean you figure on coming back? You and your mamma?"

"That's the way we planned it. That's what we always talked about, while I was working and going to school. It was what I always wanted to do, and Pa thought it was a good idea."

Israel asked, "You been going to school mostly?"

"That's right. I finished medical school three years

ago and I've been getting hospital training and experience since then."

"Lord today!" Velvet exclaimed. Both of them were excited.

"Then you's a doctor, a sure enough doctor, like Dr. Boyd, or like Dr. Anderson used to be?" Israel rose from his chair. He stood close with his hand on David's shoulder.

"And we supposed to call you 'Doctor,'" Velvet said. "Everybody got to call you 'Doctor.'"

"Oh, no," David answered. "You're like family, and I'm the same David Williams, older of course, but like you've always known me. I'm still David. When I get started with my practice I'll be Dr. Williams to the patients."

Israel went back to his seat. "Dr. David Williams," he said over and over. "I sure like the way it sound: Dr. David Williams. Velvet, don't it sound good?"

David explained that he was back to look around. He had a two-week vacation period. By the first of July he would have completed his specialty training and he would be ready. He saw there were changes. He wanted to know about them and understand. He wanted to consider locations and the needs of the people.

Israel agreed that there were many changes.

"But you'll find friends," he said. "Everybody

remembers the Williamses. And the whites too. They ain't so rebbish as they used to be. Even Old Man Boyd, he's changed, and Harold Boyd, now he's a doctor too."

"Harold Boyd? He's a doctor?" David asked.

"Sure enough," Israel said.

Velvet added, "And he's got his own hospital, Old Man Boyd built a hospital for him, had it ready soon as young Dr. Boyd came back from his schooling. You'll see."

David had good reason to remember Harold Boyd and his father. Harold was two years older than David. His father was the richest man in the county.

"If you come back here doctoring," Velvet said, "it could be the Boyds would try to give you some more trouble."

"No, they wouldn't have cause to do that," David answered. "I wouldn't be competing with Harold in his hospital. There always are plenty of sick people who need attention and there never are enough doctors. How about Dr. Anderson? Is he still around?"

They said that Dr. Anderson still lived in his house in the country but he no longer tried to serve the people.

"He's old and he's right doty," Velvet said.

They told him about other doctors in town. One, an older man, was at the Boyd Memorial Hospital. It was said he was very good, especially at operations. Another was in an office over the drugstore on Main Street. Then there was a young doctor who had been brought in by the new cotton mill. All of them were white. None of them made house calls, and they served black people only when they had time left over from their white patients.

"We truly do need a good doctor here," Velvet said, "but you think they going to let you?"

"Let me?" David laughed. He knew that fears still lay deep in the minds of some black people. "They can't stop me. I am a qualified medical doctor. I'm licensed in the state of New York. I'll just have to get my license for this state."

"Things is changed, Velvet," Israel put in. "David's right. Ain't nobody can block him once he get his license."

"These folks got ways," Velvet insisted. "I seen too much they can do, folks like Old Man Boyd and that Dr. Harold Boyd."

"Velvet, you know I used to be afraid," David said. "I was afraid of what white folks could do, but if I've learned anything, I've learned that even the meanest of them, the most rebbish, are people too. They aren't giants and they aren't great brains. Most of them are small and weak. I know I've got what it takes to deal with them. They can't hurt me."

Velvet looked at David with new wonder in her eyes. She admired his courage. She wanted to believe he could succeed, but she still had her fears.

Israel, Jr., and the girls came home on the school bus. The girls were shy. They had little to say but they were happy at the prospect of staying for several days at the farm with their grandmother. Junior was less restrained.

He gave a loud "Wow! That's neat!" when his mother said, "This is Doctor David Williams. He's a real medical doctor."

Later Junior said, "I heard about you before. You and my Uncle Ben who lives in New Jersey, you and him were good friends." And when David agreed, Junior said, "How about it . . . would you mind . . . suppose I called you 'Uncle David'?"

"I'd like that," David replied. "That's neat."

That evening David Williams sat late on the top step of the porch where he used to live. Velvet was nearby in the porch swing. Israel Crawford, also seated on the step, was giving the news. Israel, Jr., sat a little farther away. He said nothing but he seemed to be listening to everything.

Woolford, the curly-haired black house dog, snuggled at David's side. Israel said the dog recognized David as a member of the family.

Israel thought it would be good for David to settle in South Town. Velvet was not so sure.

"This ain't no place to live," she said. "Now Ben, he picked up and moved up north, him and his little family. He doing all right too. He come home every year, driving his own car."

Israel put in, "And half the time he ain't working— layoffs, strikes, shutdowns."

"But his wife working," Velvet said. "A nurse. She's a nurse working in a big hospital."

Israel turned, angry. "And Ben most and generally doing housework and taking care the little ones. What kind of man he think he is?"

"He better off than down here," Velvet answered. "Beside, her ma be with them in the house. She take care the house and the children too. And Ben ain't out of work that much."

David did not like to be in the argument. "There are lots of families in the cities like that," he said. "Sometimes the women can get better jobs than the men, sometimes better pay even, and steady. When it's like that, lots of men are willing to stay at home and do what they can there."

They talked about the way things are and the way things ought to be, with Israel and Velvet disagreeing.

"David," Velvet asked suddenly, changing the subject, "you got a wife?"

"No. I guess I've been too busy to think about getting married. Besides, with me in school and not earning any money, who would have me?"

"Don't you have nobody on your mind? Maybe a nice nurse or a schoolteacher?"

"Not now I don't, not anybody."

"If you did, you ought to talk to her real good. Looks like if she had any sense she wouldn't let you bury yourself in a place like this. She'd want city life."

David had to agree that most of those he knew wanted city life.

"Besides," Velvet said, "these country folk got no money, not no real money. Most of them don't own their own land. They still farming on shares, whites as well as blacks."

"I guess I'll find somebody someday, maybe somebody from right around here."

"That ain't likely," Israel cut in to say. "Our young folks, if they get their schooling, they take off. If they don't go north they go to some city."

"Looks like you could have got somebody by now," Velvet said with a smile. "Tell me them doctors and nurses have lots of chances to get together. Sometimes they get married, even. Didn't you have chances like that?"

"Yes. I guess I did. I had chances."

David gave Velvet only a limited account of his experiences. What he said was primarily in answer to her direct questions.

When she spoke of doctors and nurses getting

together, David knew what she meant. While he was in medical school, and before that, while he was in undergraduate school at State College, he heard talk which suggested that nurses and doctors socialized together and that love affairs developed, uninhibited and unchecked. Certainly, it seemed, the opportunities were there.

Medical school had given David the answers to many of his earlier questions about sex. Some of the things he learned were disillusioning. Some of his fellow students had gone to great lengths in satisfying their curiosity. Very few showed interest in the nurses around them.

"A nurse is not a woman," one of his lecturers had said in class. "When the doctor looks at a nurse and sees 'woman' you can know that he is losing his perspective."

Velvet went on to question David about his life before he had been so deeply involved with medical school and hospitals.

"Well, there was a girl, but that was a while ago." David smiled as he said it. Velvet leaned forward. Junior got up and moved closer.

"It was while we were both in high school," he said. "Jeanette Lenoir was her name."

"Some kind of foreigner, was she?" Velvet asked.

"No—well yes, maybe. Her folks were from New

Orleans, some kind of Creoles. After graduation from high school in North Town she went to college back in Louisiana. She's married now."

Three

After breakfast the next morning they told him how to get to the Boyd Memorial Hospital. He drove into town and up Main Street beyond the business district and over the next hill of residences.

The hospital sat on high ground to the right of the road. A large, three-story structure of light-colored brick, its architecture suggested the traditional southern mansion. Four white columns reached from the ground floor to the roof. A curved formal driveway added to the "big house" image. But David could see that the side was modern, functional in design. The emergency entrance was plainly marked. An ambulance was backed to the loading platform. On the second and third floors French doors opened to balconies, where patients were seated taking in the morning sun.

In the wide parking lot David pulled into a slot, and without locking the car he started for the front entrance. An orderly, black, met him at the door. David smiled at him as the man spoke.

"Excuse me, but visitors not allowed to park in the doctors' section."

"Yes, I understand, but I am a doctor."

"Oh, that's all right. I didn't know. Guess I didn't recognize you."

David explained that he had not been there before.

"Sure, sure, I guess Dr. Boyd will be glad to see you. I'll show you in."

Leading the way, the orderly went by the desk marked "Information" as he said to the young white woman on duty there, "This doctor wants to see Dr. Boyd."

They turned, without knocking, into a door marked "Private." A secretary looked up.

"This gentleman is a doctor," the orderly said. "He wants to see Dr. Boyd."

It wasn't the approach David would have made, but after all, he knew it was better to see the doctor before inspecting the hospital. He wished he might have looked around, just getting an informal view. He would rather observe on his own than be shown.

The secretary showed surprise.

"The name is Williams," he said, "Dr. David Williams. Dr. Boyd may not remember the name but I used to live in South Town."

The secretary, without speaking and without smiling, went to announce the visitor.

The orderly stopped at the door. "I'm glad you came back to South Town, Doctor," he said. "And I wish you would come back and stay. We need you."

Harold Boyd came out of his private office ahead of his secretary. He was shorter than David but heavier.

"Dave Williams! Doctor David Williams! Great God almighty! Man, come in. Come in. Always knew you'd make it! Wait 'til I tell the folks."

Dr. Williams had his congratulations to offer, too. He knew that even with the money the Boyd family could put behind him, Harold Boyd could not have made it through college and medical school without hard work and steady application. It was an accomplishment for anyone, even a rich student. David knew, also, that the family could establish Harold in a modern health facility but it would take work, and dedication, to keep it going effectively.

Harold Boyd kept asking him questions, hardly waiting for answers, about high school after leaving South Town, undergraduate work, medical school, internship, residency.

"And on time, man. No lost time at all. And now you come back to look around the old stomping grounds. Well, I have to tell you that the world has changed a lot. South Town, the whole state, the whole South is not the same."

Harold took David's arm and led him from the room, stopping to tell his secretary, "This boy used to work for my dad, and his daddy did too, and I guess his ma used to work for my mother. Great Day! What a connection."

"And now he's a doctor? A regular medical doctor, a physician?" the secretary asked.

"Well, soon will be anyway. And the black doctors up north make a pile, maybe more than the white medics."

Harold led the way through the well-furnished office and stopped in the center of the outer lobby, pointing to the comfortable waiting room which might have seated a score of persons.

At the desk a young black girl in a white dress was putting cards into a file. Beyond her a white nurse sat at a table. They both looked up and smiled. They seemed to know that Dr. Boyd was with a special guest.

"You've got to know my number one staff assistant," he said as he opened a door with a name plate: "Dr. Von Schilling." A woman, obviously a patient, was about to leave.

"He's a foreigner," Harold said to David, "but he's a really great, great surgeon, probably best in the state."

Almost before the patient was out of the room Harold was saying, "Dr. Von, look what we have here. Would you believe a black boy who used to work in

my daddy's garage—now he's through medical school
and about ready to go to work."

Dr. Von Schilling, white-haired, thin, but as tall as
David, put out his hand.

"Welcome, Doctor," he said with a heavy European
accent, "welcome. We need more doctors, and I'm sure
that right here we need more staff, full time."

"I don't think old Dave would want to stick around
here. He'll probably big-time it up north. That's where
the money is, especially for a black doctor."

David was annoyed that Harold Boyd would pre-
sume that a black doctor, any more than a white,
would want to be where the money was.

Von Schilling answered before David spoke. "But
the need," he said. "And I don't believe that a man
who takes his oaths seriously will think only of the
money he can make."

"Well, you know how they are," Harold cut in.

"That's the way I feel about it," David said. "I've
always thought about coming back, all the time I was
away—every time I thought about becoming a medical doctor I thought it would be right here that I
would practice."

"So you see," Von Schilling said.

Harold said quickly, "But here? I hadn't thought
about that—still, maybe it would be good for us to
have a black doctor on staff. We get some funny
situations with people. Most of them are ignorant and

superstitious, you know, even the white ones, lots of them. Yes, I guess that would work out, maybe a special wing, with your own waiting room. Not segregated, of course, but they would naturally want to go to you. That might be all right."

"Special wing?" David said, moving toward Harold. "Special ward? Let's understand—I am a doctor and the license I hold is not for a special wing or a special waiting room."

"That's right. This man is a doctor," Von Schilling said. "The hospital couldn't shunt him off in a separate department, or a wing. We need him here in full line of duty."

Harold raised his hand and stopped the older man. "You don't understand, Dr. Von," he said. "You don't know how it is. We do take in blacks and you know we don't segregate them, not really. That's the law, the federal law. But David knows, he knows we can't put our best people under the care of a Negro. They wouldn't put up with it, hardly none of them. Men maybe, but they wouldn't let a black man touch their women, and we're not going to try to go that far."

"Never mind," David said quickly. He was hearing too much. He wanted to get away before he exploded. "Never mind. You won't have to worry about me. I wouldn't want to come into your setup."

"It's a good setup, Dave," Harold insisted. "We treat everybody right and we don't segregate, but you can't change the deep-down feelings of people by passing some laws—it takes time, man—"

"I'll not try to change your customs or your feelings," David answered, "but in all my training and experience I never found a race problem under the skin. Inside all my patients were the same, all born the same way, all subject to diseases and responding to the same cures when we had them."

"Yes, yes," Von Schilling was saying, while Harold kept shaking his head from side to side.

"It's not like you think," he said, "but we have to face facts, deal with reality."

David went on, "I'd never be willing to come in here to work in a special unit. In fact, I mean to set up my practice in this county somewhere near South Town. I want a place where the people can get to me. Those who will need me and want me. I believe there'll be plenty like that."

"Now look here, Dave Williams," Harold Boyd said, "I'm not saying we could use you here, even if you did want to cooperate, but you have to know setting up a decent place like you're talking about is not easy. You don't just do it. Why, my old man put together almost two million dollars on this hill, the physical plant plus the equipment, X rays, laboratories, operating rooms, and nurseries. It's just about meeting the needs of the community, too. You could never set up anything like this, but like I said, you ought to stay with Negroes up north, they can support you, and I bet they need what you got to give as much as these black folks here."

It was not a happy visit. The three men walked back to Harold's office. Their talk was on the edge of argument. In answer to Von Schilling's questions David reported on his own medical training, his status and experience as intern and resident at Bellevue Hospital in New York.

Before he left the two men there, Harold advised him yet once again to go back up north—New York, Chicago, or anywhere—and settle down where he could make a decent living and still be serving his people.

Von Schilling shook his hand. "I know how you feel, Dr. Williams," he said, "I understand, but I wish you could come on staff here. There is so much, there is so much."

Four

When young Dr. David Williams, intern, had first arrived at Bellevue he felt that he would never get the drift of the work. There was too much of it, too much changing of assignments. He was starting at the bottom. Everybody was bossing him, running him, telling him what had to be done right away. He was in a sweat during the eight hours assigned to him and he never got away at the end of what they called his shift. Many days, and some nights, he worked until he was dizzy with fatigue.

Sometimes, when he finally left the floor or the ward or the hall or the lobby, to get some rest, he was so tired that he could hardly make it to the room he shared with Dr. Stern, his "old lady." The room itself was designed for one intern—one chest of drawers, one table, and one chair—but two beds were there.

"It's not like we needed chairs," Stern had said the day he arrived. "They tell me you won't have a chance to sit down. Man, when you get in here you flop, hit the sack, pass out. You never fool around sitting up."

Doctors and nurses getting together? He should laugh.

Most of the nurses were older women, cold, mother types. And hard. They went about their work swiftly and efficiently, with more to do than they could possibly manage.

Getting together?

When he did think about nurses at all, it was with the feeling that nurses knew more about caring for patients than he did. They were sure of themselves. They knew what to do. The nurses ran the hospital. They engineered the operations. Even the senior medical men depended upon them for help and advice. Interns were blabbering babes by comparison. Interns were nothing. At the end of a year interns emerged to some extent. They were accepted more as individuals. The residents, a notch higher than interns, had more status, but even residents depended to a large extent on the nurses. At Bellevue about one in every four among the interns stayed on as residents. The senior residents, one in every ten residents, were top men, specialists.

A resident would seldom talk with interns except to order them around as helpers. A senior resident hardly as much as spoke to an intern.

"Get an intern to put up some more beds in this hall," a senior resident would say to a resident.

On Saturday nights they always had to put up more beds. Intern Williams could not understand, not at first anyway, why the senior residents didn't have the orderlies put up more beds during the day.

"It's simple," Stern told him. "The orderlies are organized. They got a union. They work their hours and they go home. And another difference between orderlies and interns: The orderlies get paid."

Interns worked for experience. Interns were learners. They were like apprentices and they worked long hours. They did the dirty work and carried the heavy load. The senior residents gave them assignments. The residents gave them orders. The orderlies worked swiftly and tried to avoid interns.

David learned more from the nurses than he did from the doctors who were his superior in rank.

One was Miss Jenkins.

"Jenks," she said the first time he spoke to her. "Just call me Jenks, Doctor."

She was head nurse in a men's surgical ward.

She was commander-in-chief of her territory. The senior resident showed respect for her ability. He often asked her opinion, and it seemed to David that he never told Jenks what she should do.

Jenks was past middle age. She was tall for a

woman, taller than most of the nurses, and she was muscular. She gave the appearance of being hard and firm if any one would dare to touch her. No one did.

All the doctors—residents and interns—liked Jenks. She never scolded them but she was constantly correcting them, not telling them they were wrong but suggesting better ways to do their varied tasks.

One of David's first tasks was to change dressings. He tried to remember instructions. In med school he had done the same thing on plastic dummies, and on field trips he had watched others perform in hospitals. But this duty was not the same. These were real bodies. They were his responsibilities, and worst of all there were so many of them. On his first day he could not move swiftly. He saw a nurse's aide looking at him and she was laughing. He trembled. His patients fussed. He sweated. The sight of blood and the smell of urine and fecal matter was sickening.

Where blood had come through the wound it had dried and crusted. It made the dressing stick. He tried to ease it off, hoping to relieve the pain.

In the surgery division practically all the patients had dressings, in varying degrees of complexity. He knew that these patients were paying nothing, or very little for their services, and he had been taught that this should make no difference to those who sought to restore health. It was a beautiful ideal, but under the pressures of a large city hospital with crowded facilities and insufficient staff, the level of patient care was very low. There was no deliberate neglect but there were not enough staff people and there was not enough time to meet everyone's needs.

David had to learn to work faster. Besides changing dressings, he was told to draw blood for samples and to write up case histories of patients: current complaint, prior related symptoms, other illnesses, childhood diseases, history of the health of parents, and questions about grandparents. Very few patients could answer questions about their grandparents or even their parents. Some of the patients resented the questions, but the answers had to be sought. The intern could leave out nothing, and David felt he could never get it all down—this one and the next one and the next one.

In his second week he could feel that he was learning. He stopped worrying about the unanswered questions. He peeled off old dressings without hesitation. If a patient begged him to take it easy, he promised to do so. If another damned him for his clumsiness, he closed his ears to the cursing. He did his job. He trembled less and he did not sweat. He found that if he sprayed the dry dressing with a salt-and-water solution and left it wet for ten or fifteen minutes, it would come away easily. In washing the area of a wound or an incision he found it was best to use the least possible amount of sterile solution, just enough to free the clotted matter.

Drawing blood for samples looked easy when other people did it. He had difficulty in locating the vein. Veins of some people, especially the fleshy ones, seemed to be very small. He was sorry to have to make two or three futile jabs before he could start the dark red blood flowing into the barrel of the syringe.

One day he made several tries to get blood from the veins of a newly arrived patient who was as large, possibly as strong, and certainly as dark as he was. Each time the needle went in, the man screamed as though the pain was more than he could bear. Then he made threats about what he would do if the doctor hurt him again. David knew that it hurt but he believed it did not hurt as much as the patient said. Each time the blood would not flow the patient cursed him. Other patients in the ward were laughing and shouting profanities at both the patient and the intern. David was about to make his fifth try, or it might have been his sixth. Jenks came up and stood at his side.

"Now, Mr. Porter," she said to the patient, "you know you aren't cooperating with the doctor. If you just relax I'm sure Dr. Williams can do the job."

Mr. Porter said he wasn't hurting the doctor like the doctor was hurting him, and he figured that was plenty cooperation.

Nurse Jenkins took the needle from David's hand. With her left hand she grasped the patient's arm.

"Ah, ah, ah! There you go again," she said, "tensing

up, making all those big muscles hard. You're liable to snap a needle like that."

"Hang loose, man," someone called out. "Hang loose."

There was laughter, and the nurse said as she moved her fingers over the man's arm, "Now, you see—isn't that better? And here comes the beautiful red stuff we're looking for. Take over, Doctor."

With a full syringe of blood David heard the big man say, "Didn't hurt a bit."

Later David went to Nurse Jenkins at her station.

"You can do it just as I did," she told him, "but you have to learn to use your sense of touch, feel for the vein. A doctor has to have eyes in the tips of his fingers. Just look at your left wrist. You can hardly see the slight swelling where the veins lie under the skin. Now take the fingers of your right hand and feel for the veins. You see? But you're seeing with your fingers."

It was a lesson he was never to forget. It was especially significant with people whose skin color was as dark as veins themselves.

He wondered why they hadn't taught him that in med school.

Five

David Williams wanted to drive around and look at the country. Israel offered to go with him. Junior wanted to stay out of school and go too. It was not easy for David to explain that at first he just wanted to be alone, to really see the countryside through his own eyes, to reacquaint himself, to get the feel of it. Velvet seemed to know what he was talking about.

"There'll be plenty of time for you all to help," she said. "David Williams a doctor now. He got to examine the patient. Maybe he find out what's ailing this county. Could be he decide it's hopeless, like I say it is."

The next morning he started south on Route One. Again he was impressed with the new buildings, tidy dwellings on farms, many of them brick. The tobacco barns looked interesting. No longer were they built of logs with clay sealing the cracks between. They seemed to be not as large as he remembered them. Some were covered with galvanized metal, others with brick-figured insulation board.

Tractors were working some of the fields, furrowing or hilling up. Other tractors were waiting under their sheds. He remembered that farmers used to be careless with their equipment. It was something the farm agents would fuss about. Now it looked like farmers had learned at last. Nothing was standing out rusting in the weather.

It was rolling country. The road rose and sank to the levels of the ground, but there were no turns to right or left. At the top of one rise he could see on the next summit the large square house of the Manning family. It had been a show place when he was a boy. It was the first home that he had seen with electric wiring and such modern equipment as an electric refrigerator and a washing machine. The inside plumbing had given rise to controversy. Some of the old folk said it was indecent to have the privy in the house where people had to eat and sleep. Members of the Williams family had been good friends with the Mannings. David had heard that both Mr. and Mrs. Manning were dead, but as he approached, he wondered which of the younger Mannings would still be around.

He turned off the highway and drove by the side of the house into the back. The yard was cluttered and untidy. In answer to the beep of his horn a barefooted girl in levis appeared at the back door. She looked like she was white, but David knew she could have been a light member of the large Manning family. The face of a towheaded child appeared at the window.

She did not speak to her visitor.

"Hey, Pa!" she called, half turning her head but keeping David in sight, "come."

A man in overalls came to the door and stood beside the girl. "What you want?" he asked.

"Manning family. Al or John, or any of them around?"

"Oh, them." The man wiped his mouth on the back of his hand. "Mannings don't live here no more. But I show you."

He crossed the porch and walked out to the car. "You go on back out same way you come in and drive down the road just a little piece and turn in the first dirt road. 'Tain't far. Drive back this-a-way. You'll see John's house. Nice place. White brick. You can't miss it. You'll likely find him home."

David gave the man his thanks. He started to circle the yard to head out. The man held up his hand to stop him.

"Hey, what kind of license is that?" he asked.

"It's state of Michigan," David answered. He did not bother to say that the car was not his. It belonged to a friend.

"Boy you a long way from home, ain't you?"

"Yup." David laughed. "I guess I am, a long way from home."

Like the man said, he couldn't miss the house. John was the Manning boy who had gone to trade school to learn bricklaying and stone masonry. Now he was living in his own house of brick and stone.

Dogs set up a great halloo as he drove into the yard. Before David was out of the car John Manning came out of the house. David would have known John, but John did not recognize David. When David called out his name John let out a shout, an old-fashioned country whoop.

"Come in the house, man! Great day! Come in the house. All this time I didn't know whether you was living or dead."

John explained that he was at home alone. His wife, Marie, was teaching and their six children were in school.

"I ain't been so well," John said, holding up his hands, which were twisted and swollen at the joints. "Can't hardly work at my trade."

He explained that his mother had been dead for three years. He alone of the Manning family was still living in Pocahontas County. Tenants were working the farm.

"Yes, I went by there. The man told me where to find you."

"You didn't remember him, I reckon. One of the Travis boys, all of them poor whites. They're working the farm on shares. But tell me about yourself, and your folks. I heard your old man died. How's Mrs. Williams and Betty Jane?"

David told him about the family and said that his folks all sent regards, especially to the Mannings wherever they were to be found.

"And yourself—you look prosperous. What you been doing up north?"

"Well, I guess I'm anything but prosperous. Driving a borrowed car, for instance. I've been working some, but mostly I've been in school. You know I always did want to be a doctor."

"A doctor! So you must be in the money!"

"Well, hardly. But I'll be ready pretty soon now. I've got to finish my residency at Bellevue Hospital."

"Maybe you'll be able to do something to get my hands straightened out. They call it rheumatism and arthritis and a lot of things, but the only thing they do is give me some more pills—aspirin, I reckon."

John held his hands out again. David had to look at them. He felt them, recognizing the classic signs of rheumatoid arthritis, about which much was known but for which no cure had been found.

He expressed his sympathy, and he asked, "How long has it been like this?"

John told him that while he was in trade school he

had some trouble. They said it was because he worked with wet mortar and concrete and he wasn't careful about drying his hands or wearing gloves.

"But everybody was working along just the same," he added. "They didn't have this kind of trouble."

After he started working at the trade he kept going for several years. He built many of the new brick houses, designed them too.

He showed David through his home, upstairs and down. In the city it would not have been outstanding, but in the country, half a mile off the paved road, it was surprising.

All the rooms were large, and the furniture was good but not elaborate. A playroom had light birch-paneled walls. John snapped on the color television set and showed how the Ping Pong table could be folded up and rolled away. Four bedrooms and a tiled bathroom were on the second floor.

Back on the main floor, they sat in the playroom and talked. David expressed his admiration for the house.

"Well, I done it all myself, even the wiring and the plumbing," John said. "Course I had some helpers, digging and toting and all that, but I laid it out and I did the skill work."

"I can believe that," David answered.

"And before I got locked up with this arthritis or rheumatism or whatever you want to call it I built some of the best houses around this end of the county."

David said he had seen so many beautiful houses. John started naming the people whose homes he had built.

"Course, maybe I worked too hard"—he held up his twisted hands and shook his head—"but I made a little money and before I stopped working I built my own. I reckon it's the best of all I built, but it's mine, for me and my little family, and it was worth everything I put into it." He stopped and got up from the easy chair and started toward the kitchen.

"But look at me," he said. "It's time we was eating something, and here I am going on, but it's so good to see you, man. You don't know how good it is to see you."

David tried to say that he should be moving on, but John would not let him. He asked more questions. He was glad to know that David would be coming back to South Town.

"We sure need you," he said. "Dr. Boyd and them, they make their money. First they take the white folks that can pay, then they take on the whites who don't have much, last they treat some of us, but they don't care. We can get in the hospital, emergency and operations and like that, but they just don't care. Nobody around like old Dr. Anderson. He used to serve the people. He was one white man who treated everybody decent."

As he talked, John prepared lunch. He moved swiftly in spite of his handicap, warming up food, making coffee, and slicing fresh tomatoes. He asked questions and he answered David's. His several brothers and sisters had left South Town. They ranged from New York to Los Angeles.

They sat at the table in the breakfast nook and ate boiled ham and black-eyed peas with a salad of fresh lettuce and tomatoes.

"A real salad," David said.

David asked about the sharecroppers. "Do they do pretty well?"

"Well, I guess it's like this, sharecropping is hard. It's about as hard for white folks as it is for black—only somehow I always figure whites got more chances than black. Still and all, if you're that poor it's bad, makes no difference what color you might be."

"But up and down the road it looks like prosperity's come to the South. You used to see shacks and hungry-looking people. Now the houses are better and the folks I see don't look hungry."

"Maybe you just been driving the main highways, like Route One." John answered. "Now, you take off and drive the back roads and you'll see the shacks and shanties are still there. On a Saturday you see raggedy, hungry people walking the streets in the towns, black and white. Over around my wife's school near Willowbrook there's plenty poor folks."

"Is her school integrated?"

"Oh, yes. It's integrated—but the whites who go there are hungrier even than the blacks. That's partly because some of the whites are sending their young ones to the private schools. Those schools are mostly just a few rebbish whites trying to have classes in homes and in some of the churches. Others of the poor whites don't send their kids to school at all."

"Don't they have any laws to make parents send their children to school?"

"Laws?" John laughed. "Don't you know these folks never did give the law no mind, and when it comes to anything like going to a mixed school, the folks supposed to be enforcing the law, they're against integration anyway. They don't care a damn."

"What about welfare? Can the poor people get anything like relief? Public assistance?"

"There's a system." John was shaking his head. "It don't work, though."

"Why not?"

"Lots of reasons, I guess. Number one is that a lot of people, dirt poor though they be, consider taking county money is disgraceful. They're hungry. Their children are half starved. But they call themselves proud. Number two—and this is what Marie says— they're so hungry and underfed that they truly are sick. They can't think straight. I guess Marie's right.

Poor folks around here are sick and don't know it. I guess they're waiting for you, Dr. David Williams."

"Well, I know what hunger can do to people. And I know that people who go hungry become sick. It goes beyond plain malnutrition. It's deep."

"So, like I say, they need you, we all need you."

"I hear you now. I'll be ready soon."

"Then there's one more reason: Number three is important too. Some of the black folk, the poorest of them, think like slaves. The whites have treated them so bad that they don't dare raise up to look around. Lots of them still believe a black man's got no rights that a white man's bound to respect. Folks like that live in deep fear, saying 'yessir' and 'thank you, sir' for whatever little that they get from the folks who own the land, and never daring to question."

"But I thought all that was changed." David was finding it hard to believe John's words. "We had all the struggles and the new laws. There've been riots and fighting, fighting in the streets."

"Back off the highways, Route One and like that, lots of black folk, and lots of white ones too, don't know anything about the change. And if the folks who run things, who own the land and run the schools and the welfare programs, can help it there won't be any changes."

They finished lunch with pound cake and dandelion wine.

"My mom always made it," John said. "Us kids had to gather the dandelions, but Mom wouldn't give us no more than a taste of the wine."

John tried to delay David's departure. "Marie's going to be awful disappointed not seeing you," he said.

"I'll be back, maybe sooner than you think," David said as he walked to the car. "But there's an awful lot I got to see. I'm going up some of these back roads, see some of the people you've been telling me about, those still living the old South ways."

That evening, as they sat at the supper table, David told the Crawfords about his visit.

"And sure enough," he said, "I drove along the back roads, some of them without paving, and I saw what John was talking about."

He told them about the dilapidated houses, shanties with sagging roofs and leaning walls. The people were forlorn, thin and in ragged clothes. The children were spindly-legged. Some had swollen bellies, sure signs of malnutrition.

"And you know," he said, "I tried to be friendly. I waved as I passed. Then I stopped the car. You know, those people wouldn't even talk to me."

"I know," Israel said, and the others seemed to understand.

"But I'm a black man"—he lifted his hands and looked at the others—"I'm black, same as they are."

"You're black, but it ain't the same," Velvet said.

"You're a stranger," Israel said.

"It's just like you was a foreigner," Junior added, "or a white man. They don't know you. They don't trust you. They don't know what you want off of them."

"Or what you might want to do to them," Velvet said.

"Are they really that afraid?" David asked.

"They're poor and they're ignorant and they're scared," Israel said.

"Their kids don't go to school," Junior said, "and if they do, they don't stay. Looks like they don't learn much."

David pushed back his chair. He rose and started walking around the table as he talked. "Yes. Yes," he said. "I'm sure they don't learn much in school. Tests show that a lot of children in the public schools in the city are what they call retarded. They are slow learners or not educable, they can't learn. And you know that seventy-five per cent of the retarded and slow learners are kids who were undernourished when they were infants, one and two years old. Their brains did not develop."

"But what can you do for folks like that?" Junior said.

"I'm not sure," David answered. "I'm not sure, but they need a lot of help."

"Seems to me," Velvet said, "that most of us who live kind of decent, we don't know those folks. We'd like to help them but we don't know what we could do, and I suppose they really scared of us too."

"Yes, and as I drove around I kept wondering what kind of help they needed," David said, "and more: what kind of help could I provide. I still don't know, but I got to remembering something my daddy said a long time ago.

"It was right here in this kitchen. I must have been just about your age, Junior. We were talking about people, and he said he wanted me to get out and see and then I would know what I ought to be. Today I've been seeing, maybe I'm coming to know what I ought to be."

"Well, you are a doctor. Ain't that it?" Israel asked.

"Yes, but there's more to it than that." He had to search for the words. He wanted them to understand. "Now, all this time I've been going to school and working and planning to come back. I was thinking I could help cure some sick people and maybe set some broken bones and maybe do some operations and help women have their babies. I've been thinking about doing these things, but that's not enough. There's more to it than that. Today I saw folks who are afraid of me. I can see that I have to be able to more than do for them. I've got to *be* for them. I'll have to get out there, off the highway, back in and with the sorriest and the

neediest. I've got to be with them. They have to know
that I am with them, or I'll never be able to help them,
really."

He stopped talking and walking and turned toward
the table. "Junior," he said, "do you know what I'm
talking about? Do you know what I mean about being
with the people, about being for them rather than
doing things for them?"

Junior answered, "I'm not sure, Uncle David. Tell
you the truth, I can't say I rightly understand."

Israel and Velvet said they could understand, but
Velvet said that it would take a long time and there
was so much to be done, not only with the folk who
needed help but with just about everybody else too.

"Yes, Velvet," David said. "When I first thought
about being a doctor I used to think about going into
the county seat and to the state capital, maybe even to
Washington, to talk for the people. If I be with them
and for them, then I will be able to do that."

"And there's plenty more like those you saw today,"
Israel said. "Maybe they don't all have the same
problems exactly, but they're poor and they're ignorant and most of all they're scared."

"We know what fear can do to people," David said,
"to individuals and to a community."

"Did you get over by White Creek?" Israel asked.
David said he guessed he hadn't.

"It's all rich bottom land, and the folks, the black

ones, are the poorest in the county. The land all belongs to whites now."

"Oh, I remember about White Creek," David said, "but our people used to own all that land. They had a lot of money, just came out of there to sell their crops, cotton and tobacco."

"That's right," Velvet said. "That's the way it used to be, but one way or the other whites own everything down there now—bought them out, scared some out, and killed a few that was supposed to be bad. Now all the land is under sharecropping and day labor. They raise big crops but they got machines to do the work. Tractors and cotton-picking machines."

"Owners don't need many hands to do their work," Israel said. "The blacks that be humble and slave-like can stay. The others, the owners call them trouble-makers, and they put troublemakers off the land. That's where the folks are really poor."

"Well, they must get enough to eat," Junior said, " 'cause the kids from down there sure like to fight. They go for bad. When they come in town, mostly Saturdays, they stick together."

"Don't they come in for school?" David asked.

"I guess they got a grade school down there," Junior answered. "I don't think any of them go to high school. They'll be working, making crops, by the time they're old enough. They just get to be plantation hands."

"That's what they call them," Velvet said, "plantations. And that's about what they are. Old Man Boyd owns a lot of land down there, two or three plantations."

"Uncle David, I just don't see how you can help folks like them," Junior said.

"Well, Junior," David said, "we'll have to work on it. Things do change, and people change their goals, their ways of thinking. Some of our people, like in White Creek district, seem to be slipping, losing their land, and all. But some are prospering. Some kids are going to school, learning to deal with the problems. There are ways to help, and the beginning is to understand, to understand the people, their problems, the world they live in. There are ways to help."

For a while no one spoke. They seemed to be thinking. Then David continued, "You know I'm coming back. I'm going to be working with the people. In time I'll know them, and I'll understand them. I'll find ways that I can help them to help themselves. I'm sure I will."

Six

When the word got around that the son of Ed Williams had returned to South Town, it stirred memories. People remembered when the Williams family, Ed and his wife and David and the young girl, Betty Jane, had lived in the neat white house four miles out of South Town on the main road going south.

They remembered about the time of "the trouble." That was what they called the series of events just before Ed Williams sold out and took his family up north.

It couldn't be called a riot. It wasn't simply a shooting.

It was in the days when black people were beginning to speak up for their rights, to talk back to whites. Ed Williams, who was a good auto mechanic, refused to work any longer for the pay of a helper. He demanded to be paid the same as the white mechanics.

Ed Williams had told sixteen-year-old David what happened that day.

"Mr. Boyd said I must think I'm a white man, and that the niggers were getting uppity, and that we had to be put back in our place. Then he said he wasn't going to pay me no more and he was going to fix it so I couldn't get work no place in the county. He said I'd come crawling back begging for a job, but I told him I'm a man same as him. I ain't crawling for nobody."

Ed Williams did not crawl. He never crawled. But that day, white-and-rich Boyd charged that black-and-poor Williams had threatened him. That was all it took. Williams was arrested and taken to jail. White men got together to teach all the blacks to stay in their place. They took up the old night riders' plan, to burn down the house in which the so-called troublemaker lived.

But blacks got together too. They prepared to defend the home. They gathered there with their guns. David could still remember the terror of that long night.

Israel Crawford was there, newly come home from veteran's hospital. He had his gun but wasn't yet used to having only one arm.

The cars came out from town, moving slowly. They were without lights and they stopped on the road in front of the house. The house was dark, but men were waiting inside and crouching in the bushes and lying in the ditch. That's where Israel was, and from there his voice boomed out.

"We ready for you!" he shouted. "Oh, yes—we ready. Ain't nobody scared. Can't die but once, and if we die we dies like mens and if I die you dies with me. . . . Ain't going be no house burning tonight . . . and no more lynching neither. We fighting back.

"We ready, white man, so get going or get back. And God damn you for the nasty low-down crackers you be, move out now, else I start shooting."

They had moved. The cars went up the road. The curses of Israel and others trailed in the air behind them.

It looked like it was over. Those who had been on guard left their posts. Israel joined the others inside the house. It was something like a celebration. Suddenly a burst of gunfire shattered the quiet and crashed through windows and splintered walls, and then the cars were speeding off toward the town.

One man in the house was killed, shot clean through the head. Later the sheriff and his men, supported by state troopers, arrested all those who had been in the house, including David's mother and his young sister. From the state capital and from New York, reporters and photographers gathered in South Town. Lawyers, some white and some black, came from the N.A.A.C.P. and from other civil rights organizations. Those who had been arrested were released. Ed Williams was brought home by old Dr. Anderson. Williams had been beaten. His face was swollen. His hair was matted with dried blood. He never fully recovered from the beating the whites gave him while he was held in jail.

Dr. Anderson had advised Ed Williams to leave South Town and go north— He advised it and then urged that the family leave especially for the sake of education for David, who had already said he wanted to become a doctor. The family left, but their friends never forgot them.

The three Crawford girls, Angela, Jocelyn, and Ruth, did not immediately accept David as "uncle." They spoke shyly and they used the term "Dr. Williams." They stayed out of his sight most of the time, but they were curious. They returned to the house one afternoon and helped their mother prepare food for dinner.

Before they sat down to eat the girls had very little to say, but as they ate they lost some of their shyness. Ten-year-old Ruth, the youngest, was first to speak out. She announced that she was going to be an actress.

"Or at least a singer," she added.

"That girl's a regular clown," Velvet said. "She can dance and twist about and keep everybody laughing. Gets her lessons from TV, I reckon."

Ruthie knew the names and the vital statistics of the top black entertainers, including the big money they were making.

"I keep telling my young ones," Israel said, "that money ain't everything."

Velvet did not dispute her husband, but she said she was very sure that money, and enough of it, was sure important to living decent.

Angie, fourteen years old, said she wanted to be a nurse.

David expressed hearty approval and then asked, "But have you thought about going on and becoming a doctor?"

The girls were surprised at the idea. Angie said, "Who—me?"

Junior said, "Boys get to be doctors. Girls are supposed to be nurses."

"That's a mistaken idea." David held up his hand and shook his head from side to side. "That's a mistake, a big one. Some of the best doctors are women. And some of the best nurses are men. In med school women stayed near the top of the class."

It was a brand-new idea for all of them. Angie said she would think about it.

Jocie, who was twelve, thought she would like to be a teacher. Junior had not thought much about what he wanted to be. He liked baseball and he did not like school.

"Not too much, anyway," he said.

By the time dinner was over, the girls were speaking to David as Uncle David.

While the girls were clearing the table and washing the dishes David said, "You know, I'd like to go see old Dr. Anderson."

"I can take you there, Uncle David," Junior was quick to say.

"Well, I reckon he won't need help finding the place," Velvet said, "but like as not Dr. Anderson won't even know you."

"You might be right," David said. "Just the same, Israel, if you don't need Junior tomorrow after school, maybe you could spare him to go with me to make a doctor's call on a doctor."

It was all right with Israel. Junior was delighted. He did not mind doing the work on the farm, but he wanted to spend more time with the man he was calling his uncle.

"I got my driving permit," he said, "and I can drive a VW. We had that in driver training."

"But maybe don't nobody want you to drive," Velvet said.

"Oh, the boy's a good driver, car, truck, tractor, anything," Israel said. "That is, David, if you want a chauffeur."

Junior was home from school early in the afternoon the next day. With not too much grinding of gears with the stick-shift VW, he displayed his skill at driving. He was completely at ease, and unlike some of the city boys David had seen, Junior was not a showoff. This might have been because in the country many boys operated trucks and tractors on the land long before they were old enough to hold a permit to drive on the road.

"Sometimes I think about what I want to be," Junior said, "but good grief! I wouldn't want to spend half my life in school to be a doctor."

"Well, that's one way of looking at it," David said. "On the other hand, if you want something real bad you have to give up something else to get it. I guess I just wanted to become a doctor. I always did, even before I knew how long it would take."

"How long did it take, Uncle David?"

"Let's start after high school. Four years in college to get a bachelor's degree, then four years in medical school. Then there's a year of work in a hospital as an intern and after that at least one year in residence at a hospital. For some of the specialties it can be several years. For surgery it can be four or five. I'm taking two years for family practice."

"Wow! I'd never make that."

"I bet you could. You wouldn't, though, if you just worried about how long it was taking. Maybe life is like that. We only live one day at a time, you know?"

"You're right, but four years and one and two

more"—Junior was counting on his fingers and had to go from his right hand over to his left, shifting his hold on the wheel—"good grief, that makes seven years on top of college. I'd never make it."

"Oh, it's not so bad as all that. What grade are you in now?"

"Just finishing tenth. The way our schools are that's the first year in senior high school."

"Now, you see you've been in school for ten years already. Suppose at first grade you had said, 'Ten years, and twelve to get out of high school—I'll never make it.' But you make only one grade at a time. And some of it is fun."

Junior nodded as he said, "Well, look at it like that, one grade at a time."

"And don't forget we live one day at a time."

Dr. Anderson was in a wheelchair on the front porch. Books were on a table at his side. He folded a newspaper on his lap as David got out of the car and walked up the steps. Junior followed him but he did not go up on the porch.

David Williams told Dr. Anderson who he was. At first the old man could not remember. As David repeated the name he said, "You might remember my father, Ed Williams. We used to live on Route One."

"Yes, yes, the Williams boy. You all went away after the trouble. Up north. I remember. How was it? You all made out, didn't you?"

"Well, I reckon we did, for a while anyway. My mother's well, but my father died last year."

"I guess what happened didn't do your daddy any good. But that was the last bad trouble we ever had around here. Maybe folks are learning to live together, what little time we got to live on this earth, what time we can move about, and do something worth while. It's little enough at best. That's what I always did say, and now it seems to be even truer."

"But I've seen lots of people in wheelchairs, going right on doing their work." David was trying to sound hearty.

Dr. Anderson shook his head from side to side. "Not for me," he said. "I'm through, at least so far as practice of medicine is concerned. It's not only that I can't get around. My thinking is not what it ought to be if I'm going to be holding people's lives in my hands. No. I'm through. I'm just looking back, and remembering what happened a long time ago, but looks like I can't remember yesterday. That's my problem. Remember fifty years ago, and forgetting what happened yesterday."

There was a sound of sadness in the old man's voice.

"But you've had an awful lot of experience," David said. "You could help by advising. I guess it's true that there is no substitute for experience."

Dr. Anderson gave a snort or a grunt or a sneer as he said, "Nobody wants advice from a has-been. That

young fellow with his new hospital in South Town—
would he ever think of asking me anything, or asking
about me? Nope. He good as told me even before he
got out of school, he told me 'It's all by the book.' He
thinks experience is worthless. He wouldn't ask me for
any advice, even if I could tell him something, and
maybe I couldn't."

"I'm sure you could."

"I was just an old-fashioned country doctor. My
patients came to see me right here, if they could.
Mostly I went out to see them, on the farms, owners
mostly. Tenants never called me unless somebody was
about dead. Generally it would be too late.

"I had an office in town, upstairs over the drugstore.
I'd be there after dinner on Wednesdays, that was all.
Not many folks came in. Right here, here was where
they looked for me, or came to call me. Too many
times they would call me too late. They didn't have
much money. Lots of times they gave me some fresh
eggs, maybe a bag of potatoes or a couple of chickens."

"I'm sure you helped them, though," David said. "I
remember that everybody said you were a fine doctor,
and you sure helped my folks, more than by doctoring."

"One thing: Nobody ever did sue me for malprac-
tice. I guess they knew I did the best I could."

The old man's eyes closed but he was smiling. His
head fell forward. David took a step nearer. He put his

strong hand over the withered white hand of Dr. Anderson. The skin was like parchment, lying loosely over the thin bones.

"Yes, I remember Ed Williams," Dr. Anderson said as he raised his head and looked at the strong young man bending over him. "I remember Ed Williams. And he had a boy, maybe fifteen or sixteen, something like that. Boy was right smart too. Said he wanted to get his schooling and learn to be a doctor. Yep, I reckon he made it too."

His eyes closed and his head fell forward again. The doctor was asleep.

David Andrew Williams, M.D., did not awaken him.

"Say, Uncle David," Junior asked when they were back in the car on the way home, "did you ever think about being a preacher?"

"Nope. Never thought about being a doctor of divinity. Always wanted to be a doctor of medicine."

"Well, you're about to make a convert out of me."

Seven

On Saturdays the Crawfords always went to South Town.

"I like to go early and get through," Velvet said, "but Israel likes to hang around and talk with everybody from everywhere, Brown's Cafe and Skipwith's and all."

"So most and generally," Israel said, "I take her in and bring her back, then I go back to town and take care of my business."

"And you call that business?" Velvet asked.

"Yeah," Junior cut in, "nothing happens in the morning. Only later, late in the day and more at night, everything is jumping."

"And that's when my boy don't hang around," Israel said with emphasis. "Junior ain't to be in town after dark on no Saturday night and he knows it."

"Aw, they think I'm a baby."

David realized that the talk was like a tape recording of conversations when he and his folks lived in the house. Saturday night in town was bright and loud and exciting, but he was seldom there to enjoy the thrills. There was dancing at Brown's and at the other cafes. They had licenses to sell beer and wine. Some folks always drank too much. Arguments flared up. Often people got to fighting, even women got into it. Sometimes, not too often but sometimes, there was a killing.

After breakfast David rode with Israel to the home of Israel's mother. He had not seen Mrs. Crawford, but she knew he was back. The old frame house he remembered was still there, but it showed evidence of repairs and it was nicely painted.

He remembered the mother of Israel and his good friend Ben as a sturdy farm woman, stout but not fat. She must have been strong, for she worked hard in the fields from "can" to "can't," as they said in the country, and more hours in the home.

She hugged him and kissed him and told him she hoped he would come back to stay.

"And Israel tells me your mamma be coming back too," she said. "Lord, my cup shall sure runneth over when I see Sister Williams."

Israel loaded his mother and the three girls into his station wagon and drove back to pick up Velvet and Junior. David offered to drive his own car, but the others insisted that he stay with them.

The girls were relaxed. David felt he was truly accepted by the family.

Angela asked about nurses and lady doctors in the hospitals. Ruthie asked his opinion about singers and musicians, some of whose names he had never heard before.

"I guess you don't think I am with it," he said.

"Oh, no, Uncle David," Jocie said, "she just thinks you're an old man."

Velvet said they were talking foolish. Mrs. Crawford was more positive.

"Why, he's only a boy," she said, "no older than my baby boy Ben."

David knew that didn't prove anything.

Israel parked the station wagon in the free parking lot on Main Street. Everybody was to be back in two hours for the ride home. They scattered. Angie went with her mother, Jocie with her grandmother, Ruthie with her father, and Junior said he would be showing Uncle David around.

David told Junior that first he wanted to go to Brown's Cafe, hoping to see Al Brown.

"I was there the other day, but his mother told me he was teaching school over in Jefferson County. He's supposed to be home on weekends."

Al was there. He was David's age. At one time they had been close friends. They had little time to talk because conversation was interrupted by questions and details having to do with the expected rush of Saturday business.

But Al Brown did tell David about plans for the evening. "Some of us are getting together out at Mannings'," he said—"you know, some of your old friends and some others in our crowd. I can stop by for you at about eight. I'll get away from here."

David agreed quickly. He supposed this would be a fun thing, and he wanted to see more of the people his own age. When they assembled for the ride home, Israel and Velvet heard the news without enthusiasm.

"That's a wild bunch," Israel said. "Al Brown and his crowd, supposed to be educated, all of them been to college, and I guess they got good jobs, but looks like to me they don't know how to live."

"What Israel means," Velvet put in, "is them folks don't do no hard work. They don't plant nothing and they don't have to wait for a crop. They know how much they making on their jobs and they not worried about the weather. Looks like to me they do truly know how to live. They sure have more fun than we do."

"That ain't the point." Israel tried to make it clear that he felt people should be able to plan and look ahead, to save something and to have a piece of land with a house on it and a family living there "permanent."

In the afternoon Israel went back into town to take care of his business. David spent time with the family, enjoying an exchange of ideas with Junior and the girls. He concluded that they were all smart and that each of them could reach whatever goals they might set for themselves.

He particularly wanted to know how school integration was working out.

"There was lots of talk about it for a long time," Junior told him. "We heard about the lawsuits and all the court decisions, but nothing happened here until about three years ago. Then they had some citizens' meetings. My pa went to some of them, but folks always said he was a hothead, they didn't want to listen to what he had to say, so he stopped going.

"All of a sudden it happened: They said the white high school was going to be for everybody, white and black, but it would be a senior high, and the high school that had been for blacks, the East Side High, would be a junior high school and it would be for everybody. Well, that was something!"

"Yes. I know it was," David said. "What happened?"

"Nothing." Junior was shaking his head from side to side. "They said it would begin with the new school year in September, and it did. Would you believe nothing happened? We just went. Everybody went.

The classes were all mixed up, the teachers were all mixed up, and everybody started settling down to study."

"Weren't there any fights? Didn't some of the parents make trouble?"

"You know, if it hadn't been for the parents there wouldn't have been any trouble at all. Some of the rebbish white parents took their kids out of school. And some that didn't take them out tried to make their kids feel they didn't have to go to gym with black kids or they didn't have to share anything, like science equipment, or sit with them at workbenches or eat with them in the lunchroom. But it was only the parents. We got along fine."

"How did you feel about it, yourself, Junior?" David asked. "How did you take it on? It must have been new and different."

"Tell you the truth, Uncle David, I was scared, you know. I don't like to admit it, but I was. You see, we had always been told about how smart the white kids were, how superior white folks were, and all that, you know what I mean?"

"Yes, Junior, I truly do know."

"Well, you know, us that was black, thought them white kids were going to be running rings around us in class, knowing all the answers and making us feel embarrassed, but you know what happened? We soon saw the whiteys didn't know any more than we did.

Some of them were smart, yes, but most of them were just about like most of us, and plus, we had some smart ones too. Man, when we found that out, some of us, my friends, Crutchfield and Johnnie Skipwith—some of us got together and we most died laughing."

David could appreciate everything Junior was saying because it was a reflection of what he had learned when he first went to an integrated high school in North Town.

He told Junior about his own experiences and then he asked, "How is it working out now?"

"No trouble. Principal at the senior high school is a white man and he has a black assistant principal. Principal at the junior high school is a black man and he has a white assistant. I guess people still think it's important to keep up that kind of color balance—'racial ratio' is what they call it. It won't be long, though, before folks will be putting all that behind. They'll want the best man for the job. In school students are already talking about it, and we'll be running things soon. You'll see. Everybody will see."

Eight

When Al Brown picked him up to go to the party that evening, David was glad to go.

As Al drove into the yard, David was standing on the steps talking with Junior. Junior made David think of himself when he was fifteen years old. It seemed to him, though, that Junior was much more developed than he had been. Well, David figured, Junior had more ways of learning about and seeing the world.

When they were in the car Al Brown said, "Sure enough, everybody's coming. All who were around when you were here. Of course some of them, lots of them, really, have gone away. And then there'll be some new folks. But everybody wants to see you—the old ones, and the new ones too, they want to meet you."

"But I hope you'll be calling their names," David said, "because I find that some of them I really don't remember."

"I know how it is—'Remember the face but forget the name' sort of thing."

David laughed. "No, it isn't even that," he said. "The faces have changed, and even when I get the name I just don't remember the person. In fifteen years I've seen a lot of faces and heard an awful lot of names in a great variety of situations. I just don't remember most of them. John Manning told me about the girl he married. He told me her name, one of the Slaughters, and I guess I ought to remember her but I don't."

"I guess you're right. Besides, she was a little girl when you left and she's a woman now, teacher, mother of half a dozen kids. Yes, I'll try to remember to call the names of people."

The car turned off the paved road. As they approached the brightly lighted house, David could see many cars parked on the side of the road.

"Looks like the party started without waiting for the guest of honor," Al said as he worked the car into a parking space by a vine-covered fence. Some of the guests had spilled out to the front porch and the yard. As David stepped out of the car, the old fragrant smell of lilacs was heavy in the warm night air. The sound of voices and of music reached him. Al led the way.

They were greeted cheerfully. John Manning himself stepped forward. He reached out his twisted hands to take David's shoulder.

"Welcome, man!" he shouted. "Looks like I had to

bring the whole county together to get you back into my house, but that's all right. My wife and all the kids are waiting, and so are the others."

There were outstretched hands as he moved in. Most of the furniture which David had seen had been removed for the party. The place was crowded. Few faces were familiar, but as the crowd closed around him many of them called their own names, and memories of school, neighbors, and the Oak Grove Baptist Church came back to him. He would not have known John Manning's wife had not John shouted as she approached, "You remember Marie. She was the prettiest gal in Chase City." Just the same David acted as though he remembered, and when she opened her arms in welcome he went to her and kissed her on the cheek.

Then there were others, gathering around him calling out their names, identifying as wives and husbands, and sons and daughters, of people whose family names were familiar.

After the first hearty reception David was able to see that many others had not come forward. They were the ones he did not know, and ones who had never known him. Among these he was surprised to see several white people.

He would not have been surprised to see such mixing in homes where he had been living, but he had not expected to find so much change in the area of South Town.

They gathered around, and with the introductions he learned that one of the white guests, John Smith, was principal of South Town Senior High School. His wife, Peggy, a petite blond, was a teacher in the school with Marie Manning. Peggy and Marie were the best of friends, and Peggy was helping with the serving of refreshments. Another white man, Ackerman, affectionately nicknamed Tex, was from Texas. He was the county farm agent, especially interested in improving the strains of livestock in the state.

A smiling young woman was at a glass punch bowl which was overflowing with a creamy liquid. She filled a plastic cup and handed it to David. It was indeed creamy, foamy, and as he tasted he recognized it.

"Eggnog!" he said.

"Yes, I know. And you are surprised," the pretty woman said. "I remember when I first came. In the North we have eggnog only during the winter holidays. Here they use it all the year, especially at a welcome home party, and that's what this is."

"Well, eggnog at this time of year is something different, but it's all right."

"And made with country corn! That's another difference, isn't it?"

Others were cutting in with remarks and this girl

was being pushed aside, but she added as they were separated, "I'd like to talk to you about the differences."

John Manning wanted to know whether David had made up his mind about coming back to South Town. His wife assured him that everybody wanted to see him come back and she called on Peggy Smith to back up her opinion. Peggy and her husband, the school principal, agreed that this would be the best thing that could happen to South Town.

"You have to understand," Smith said, "that our problems have been worked on but they haven't all been solved yet. Your coming here as a practicing physician would say something to everybody."

"Well, I wouldn't want to come just to say something," David was surprised to hear himself answering. "I used to think a great deal about proving something because I was black. But beyond that I think about coming here because it is home. All the time I've been away I've known that I was a country boy in the city."

"It's got to be more than that, Dr. Williams." A heavy bass voice sounded behind David. He turned and saw a very dark, bearded man. He was older than most of the others. He was bald. His thin face was lined. His eyes were deep-set. He had the look of a gaunt priest, or a magic worker or prophet. "It's got to be more than that. You can't stop proving something. You are black. That is the most important thing in your life. It's the most significant fact in all of your relationships with all other people of the world. You are one who might sublimate your Black Rage, but only for a time. You are, in the words of Fanon, one of the 'Wretched of the Earth.' You and I, and all of us here who are black, are bonded together by our blackness. Don't ever forget it."

The voice was not loud but it was forceful and commanding. Others stopped talking. David had heard such statements many times, and he knew they could lead to arguments and end only in hard feelings.

The young woman who had brought him the cup of eggnog was first to speak. "Well, Dr. Hart," she said, "I guess we could get into another black-white and love-hate discussion to take up the whole night. . . . For myself, I claim to be a human being with problems living among a lot of other human beings who also have problems. I'm working on my problems and hoping the others work on theirs. My present problem is I'm hungry, but Marie can solve that. She's got a table loaded down and this eggnog is too damn weak. Hey, John, bring in the jug." It started a laugh. "My cup is empty and the guest of honor's cup is dry. Refill everybody."

Someone handed David a cup of eggnog and then the girl brought him a plate of sandwiches, a chicken leg, and a stuffed egg.

"This is just not the time to settle the world's

troubles," she said with a laugh. "I know what Dr. Hart is saying, and to some extent what he says is true, but there's a lot more to living than fighting."

"Yes, there's healing and curing," David said, "and that's where I'm coming from."

"And there's teaching, and learning, and understanding," she said, "and that's my role."

"You teach, then."

"Yes, sociology." David was surprised to know that she was at an upper level of teaching. "I'm at the community college. It's my first big job and I'm learning more from the experience than I'm able to teach."

She went on to say that her name was Joyce Palmer. This was her first time in the South. Born in Harlem, she had grown up in a New York suburb. She had a bachelor's degree from Hunter College and a master's degree from Columbia.

"I thought that because I was black I knew all about race problems," she said, "and when I got the chance to teach in the South I thought it was just the greatest opportunity. Well, it has been. And getting to know the people provides constant surprises."

"I find that too," David answered. "Although I grew up right here it is amazing to see the changes from complete segregation."

John Smith, the high school principal, was listening. He was nodding in agreement.

"Yes, I know what you mean, Doctor. I grew up in Virginia, in a segregated school and segregated neighborhood, and truly believing that white people were especially endowed, superior to black people. But we never knew any black people. We didn't even talk with them. That was the way it was, and we just took it for granted that it had to be that way."

"Tell me, Mr. Smith," the young lady said, "how did you feel about integration of the schools?"

"Well, Miss Palmer, Peggy and I have laughed about that many times." His wife smiled beside him, nodding her head in agreement. "At first I was afraid of it. I guess I was just plain scared. I always knew that there were a lot of things wrong with the system in the South but I couldn't imagine changing. Then when the laws changed and everybody got uptight, I guess we were looking for trouble, expecting shock. We believed that the students would be lining up for fights, and that even teachers would be having problems in relationships."

"And what did happen?" David asked.

Smith said, "Nothing."

Others said that almost nothing or very little happened.

"I guess it wasn't *really* nothing," Smith said later. "We had some parents who took their children out of school. Private schools were set up. Some churches organized schools. The private schools have serious problems. Financing is only one of the problems. Standardization is another."

"I can see a class struggle too," Miss Palmer, teacher of sociology, said. "The ones coming to our campus from public high schools have made some kind of adjustment to the workings of the new South. Students from the all-white private schools are in most cases poorly adjusted. They are afraid. When they come into my class for the first time they seem to be embarrassed. I try to put them at ease, but I have to recognize their problems. Some adjust quickly. Others are unable to overcome their fears."

"We see that in the high school too," Smith said. "It's natural, a fear of the unknown."

"Let's not forget the personal problems of the black kids," Marie put in. "Since slavery days the whole system has instilled fear and insecurity in them. 'White is right,' 'White people are smarter,' and all those things have been taught and drilled into the minds of black children. It is beautiful to see them in a mixed school situation as they unfold to the realization that they can do just as well as their white classmates."

"Yes," Peggy Smith put in. "We see it working out all the time in the classrooms. It's interesting to see the white kids, too, waking up to the realization that the black kids are not that different."

The party lasted until after midnight.

David found himself taking part in discussions and answering questions.

"Do you really plan to come back and set up practice?" they asked.

His answer in each case was that he did definitely plan to return.

He received advice: "Come on. We need you."

There were a few who shook their heads in doubt. "I wouldn't do it," they said. "You won't like it."

One said, "The changes are only on the surface. You will see. Even for a man like you, a doctor, the whites will make it hard."

Nine

Certainly not everybody wanted Dr. David Williams to return to South Town. Israel and his wife were divided in their opinion. Dr. Boyd said he was not needed and that he could not succeed.

Most people who talked with him, however, said he was needed.

On Sunday he went with the Crawfords to Oak Grove Baptist Church. He and his family had been members there when they lived in South Town. By this time Israel Crawford was a deacon.

The old white-painted wooden building had been replaced by a new building of pressed brick. Electricity supplied the lighting. Windows on both sides were of frosted glass, and a round stained-glass picture window filtered soft colors over the raised pulpit area. David noticed that the burial ground just west of the church building was better cared for than it had been. No weeds were growing among the tombstones, and the ground was free of litter.

The preacher was a young man who did not know the Williams family, but he had heard about them.

Dr. Williams was introduced. Most of the people remembered him. They crowded around after the benediction to ask about his parents, his sister, and his plans.

"We sure wish you would come on home now and help us out," some of the people said. Over and over he heard complaints that often they couldn't get into town when they needed medical attention and that none of the doctors would call on them in their homes. A person sick at home might be treated with whatever the family thought was best until he or she was nearly dead. Taking the sick to the hospital in town was often the last ride.

In the afternoon people came to visit at the Crawford home. They started dropping in early, and they continued to visit until long after dark. David kept asking about the people he remembered who were near his own age. He was told that most of them, like his best friend, Ben Crawford, had gone off, a few to cities in the South but most of them to the North.

That evening David said he would like to see more of the county, perhaps the towns over in what was called the west end. It was agreed that Israel would drive; Junior would be going to school.

The next morning they drove south on Route One and then took the right turn toward the county seat. They talked about changes and developments. Israel described a new dam. The river had formed a lake, and along the shore promoters were developing boating and fishing resorts.

"Some makes money out of it and holds on to the money, maybe puts it down elsewhere," Israel said, "and some gets their money and just throws it away."

"That's old and it's new," David answered. "But the whole countryside doesn't look like what I had expected."

"I don't know what you was looking for."

"I guess I don't either. Some things are better, but some are worse too. Some progress, but still . . . I just can't explain what I was looking for and what I'm missing."

"Well, everything looks just about the same to me," Israel said. "Anyway, we coming on into the county seat. Not hardly nothing new here. Maybe some of the houses been fixed up. Everybody got electricity and inside plumbing now. But yonder is the courthouse. That ain't changed, but they built a new jail on the back. On Saturdays folks still come to town and hang around the square to meet their friends."

"But they don't come in with wagons and mules. They're driving their cars and trucks."

"Reckon that's true. Folks don't bother with a mule.

Them that has them just kind of keep them for pets, round the place. The women is sentimental and the kids like to ride on them."

Israel pulled up and stopped across the square from the courthouse. It was indeed the same. It was about the same as many other courthouses throughout the state, red brick with four white columns from the wide front porch to the overhang of the roof two stories up.

"Yonder's the hardware store," Israel said, "with the part next door, well maybe that's new, that's the tractor and farm equipment department. I bought my new tractor there. She cost me eight thousand dollars."

"I didn't know you had a tractor." David was surprised.

"Yep. Need a tractor. Oh, not on the place where we're living, but where Ma lives. I bought that old place, you know. The old man was trying to pay off the mortgage when he died. Then Boyd tried to foreclose. That's what he's done on lots of farmland, so he owns just about half the land in the county."

"You managed to hold on?"

"I got veteran rights. The others in the family signed over their rights to me. That gave me first claim on the title. Then the V.A. helped me get a new loan. It was another mortgage but it was a decent interest rate."

"Well, that's good, you can manage the payments, then."

"No. Don't have no more payments. Tobacco crops

been good. Done paid it off and got the land free and clear."

"Fine. I remember that was good land. I worked some with Ben and your folks on tobacco."

Israel laughed. "Smoking is bad. Just the same, an awful lot of people must be smoking right much. Price of tobacco is high and it goes higher every year. Looks like you doctors don't have much power with the public."

Israel explained that he had money saved to buy another farm, but prices on good land were very high. "Might catch me one at auction. Sometimes when old folks die the young ones done gone to the city, up north or somewheres. Then they wants to sell out fast and get their money. That's the best way to buy. I be ready the next time around."

"Israel, you say that land is very high?" Israel nodded his agreement.

"Then, how about a small place, say one or two acres with a house on it, maybe a place the size of yours where I could set up office?"

"Nope. My place is not up for sale. Not at no price and not even to you."

David laughed at the serious response. "Well, I wasn't thinking about making you an offer. I was just thinking about some house where I could live and make office space, maybe have to add on to get enough room."

"Of course, if we was about to sell, nobody would have a better right than you. It just so happen we is like dug in, and we like it. Besides, all the land along that stretch of old Route One is awful high-priced. There's gas stations and eating places. You wouldn't believe how much we been offered already."

"I know how it is. Believe me, I wouldn't want you to sell now, even to me." David put his hand on Israel's arm. He knew Israel was feeling a bit guilty, as though he might be standing in David's way.

"It was your daddy, David, let me have the place. It was cheap too. I knew it was a low price, but I didn't know for a long time how it should of been. But you know I can help out some if you sure 'nough decide you want to settle here."

"I'm sure that I do." David paused and said with deep thought, "It won't be like I thought it would. Maybe I won't be as useful as I dreamed I would. Perhaps I can't do as well or as much as I'd like to do. Maybe they won't let me help."

"Don't even think that." Israel was very serious. "They need you. We never had a black doctor round here. Dr. Anderson was a good man but he is wore out, plumb wore out."

"Yes. I know," David said. He told Israel about his visit.

As they drove, they talked. At each place where the highway was crossed by another paved road Israel slowed and looked at the facilities which were there. At most of them gas stations had been put in.

"The gas companies pay good money for these corners. Even if they don't put in a station, they take the land. Then they let it out to rent but they own it. Remember Stanback? He used to own over there. He got good money. Gone now. He gone up north someplace."

David was thinking as he saw the other corners. Most of the people had their own cars and could reach him as well in the country as in town. Also, and most important, he would be making house calls.

"Do you think I might be able to get a good corner somewhere, maybe with a house already standing, even back from the road?"

Israel did not know of any.

"Is there a real estate broker? Somebody who acts as agent for buyers and sellers?"

"Old Man Boyd, he the one. He owns the bank, he knows who wants to sell, and he tells them what price to get, then he tells the ones who wants to buy what price to pay. Nobody else. Some has tried to do that kind of business without Old Man Boyd, but they tell me wasn't nothing done right, not until Old Man Boyd got hold of it."

They made the circuit—the county seat, Chase City—and then started for home. They saw several houses which could have been converted into serviceable quarters for a country doctor. Some were well placed near intersections. In each case Israel described the owners as persons who were not likely to sell.

Israel struck his thigh with his hand.

"Lord, you know I plumb forgot. We just been talking about too many things." He pulled a piece of paper from his shirt pocket. "I got to pick up some things for Velvet. We done passed the big stores but we can go by Old Man Haywood's. You remember Haywood's store, just a couple of miles from our house."

David remembered. Haywood's store was on a narrow east-west road where a smaller unpaved road crossed it. Haywood gave credit. His prices were high but he had the things that people needed. They could buy and tell him to put it on the book. Sooner or later they would pay up.

"Velvet go to town on Saturday and buy up a carload," Israel said, "and come Monday she got a list again, and could be Old Man Haywood ain't got nothing she got on the list."

"Now you call him 'Old Man' Haywood. Is he really that old?" David asked as Israel headed into the side road.

"Well, he getting on." Israel was silent for a while, then he went on, "But yet and still it could be something beside age is catching up on him. Things done changed. Most everybody round here goes to town to buy. The store don't have much business. His old lady's dead too. One daughter lives with him. She ain't much use to him, can't do nothing in the store. Could be it's more than years coming down on the man making him old. You'll see."

As they pulled off the road in front of the store, the building, as well as the man, seemed to speak of old age.

The store had not been painted for a long time. Two white men sat on a bench on the wide porch. A black man sitting on the edge of the porch called a cheery greeting to Israel. The two white men also spoke to Israel, and David recognized one of them as the storekeeper.

Israel and David walked up the steps. Haywood looked hard at David.

"Boy, don't I know you?" he asked.

"This is somebody you ain't seen for a long time, Mr. Haywood," Israel said. "This here is David Williams, Dr. David Williams now. His daddy was Ed Williams. They went away."

"Yes, yes, Israel, I remember Ed and I remember this boy. Come on over. Maybe you can set a while with a old man and tell him something about what's happening nowadays in the world of man."

"David Williams is a doctor," Israel said with pride, "a real M.D., ready to cure what ails you."

"Do tell. Do tell," said the man beside Haywood. He was laughing as though he had just heard a funny story.

Haywood said, "I got plenty aches and pains. Ain't seen a doctor for a long time. Maybe I'd ought to let you look me over."

"Well, Mr. Haywood," David said, "I'm not ready yet. Not quite. Have to finish up some more work and get my license from the state board. Then I'll be ready."

"Now, that's just fine." Haywood seemed to be very pleased. He did not show surprise. "You just keep right on in that training school 'til you get your diploma. But I guess then you wouldn't be coming back down to Pocahontas County. God knows we need a good doctor, now that Dr. Anderson won't come out. They say he's too old. I say being too old is only in the mind. He's probably smart as he ever was. Just don't want to work at being a doctor now."

Israel said, "But Mr. Haywood, I heard you say that you was tired being a storekeeper around here."

"Now, you didn't hear me right. I didn't say I was tired of being a storekeeper; what I said I was tired of folks bothering me, yes sir, tired of folks—period. If I could get out of here and just work my land, work it like it ought to be worked. Forty acres, more than forty acres, I got. Most of it's growed up in pine since I been here."

"But you been had some pretty good tenants."

"Good tenants? Any tenants that's any good don't stay. Them that stays just use up the land. Don't care. If I was farming them forty acres for the years I been tending store I could be a rich man."

"Haw, now, Mr. Haywood, everybody knows you a rich man. You probably could buy all your old farming customers out any time you wanted to."

"Do tell. Do tell," Haywood's friend said again.

"Just ain't so. Maybe I worked hard to enjoy my old age. But I got some more years before I get old, least before I quit. Now I'd like to get out there on my acres and do some real farming. I'd show you all—farm agent, and them Boyds, and everybody."

"Mr. Haywood, everybody knows you got stuff for all of them."

"Yeah, they used to call me a poor damn Carolina cracker. Sure I come here from Carolina, and I'm a cracker and ain't 'shamed to say it. I come here and took over this farm and I just started the store for makeshift, something to put groceries in the kitchen for me and my family whilst we getting started making our own crops on the farm. Then I seen how much the folks around here needed a store. Like I always say, first I had the store, then the store had me."

Everybody laughed at the picture. Haywood enjoyed his own joke.

"But sure 'nough, now, Mr. Haywood," Israel said, "Velvet wants some things. I got a list."

The list called for baking powder, a box of cloves, paper napkins, and some bottles of cold drinks. The store was out of cloves and paper napkins. They had plenty of colas and ginger ales.

David was looking around while Israel made his purchases. The place was gloomy, the shelves nearly empty. The ceiling was high. At one time goods had been stored overhead. The cross beams were nearly empty now. Ropes twisted in and out of the rafters. Near the front door hung a section of block-and-tackle rigging. Its iron hook was coated with rust. Faded posters and old calendars covered the walls. Through a window open at the back, David could see Haywood's home. It was a boxlike frame building of two stories. A woman sat in a rocking chair on the porch.

David was glad to hear Israel's question.

"Mr. Haywood, is you sure 'nough thinking of getting rid of the store and working your farmland? Farming do seem to pay right well these days."

"Yes, by God, that's what I want to do. That's what I was talking about only this morning. My friend who was here, he got land, doing all right on it too, and still he ain't working too hard. He got a tractor and he uses hired hands. Now, I tell you that's living."

Israel looked at David and nodded. David spoke.

"Mr. Haywood, ever think about selling out some of your land, maybe two or three acres with the store?"

"Sure enough. That's just what I been thinking," the old man said with a smile. "I been thinking about that for maybe ten years." Haywood made a wide sweep with his arm. He looked out toward the front and said, "I used to sell right smart gas. Lots of cars go by here. You'd be surprised how many cars go by here. Corner too. They turn here going to Chase City and all. Somebody liable to come along and buy me out, buy this whole corner, put in a gas station, maybe Standard or Texaco. They pay good money for a corner like this."

David heard Israel grunt. It was like he had been struck in the abdomen. David himself felt the impact of Haywood's words.

Israel said it. He spoke up to say that the big companies weren't buying on any of the back roads. They went for the highways, corners close to the national highways like the replacement for Route One. Why, even on old Route One, which had carried big business, many of the service stations had closed up, couldn't make enough to keep open.

"You can't tell though," Haywood insisted. "Say Standard put in a good big station right here on this land, then maybe Mobil open one across the road. Pretty soon you see more cars going through here. The state paving and widening to take care of the traffic. It could happen. That's what I been thinking about."

"No, man, no. It ain't like that." Israel was speaking slowly as he shook his head from side to side. "That ain't the way it is. The traffic don't follow the service station. The gas company don't put no station in to pull the traffic. The gas company go where the traffic already is at. The way it is, the service stations is following the cars. Ain't nobody going to buy this place off of you for a service station."

Haywood's shoulders drooped as Israel talked. He walked over and leaned against the doorway, looking out.

Israel said, "If that's what you waiting for, you can forget it." He kept talking until David felt sorry for the old man.

When Israel stopped, Haywood raised his head. He looked from Israel to David and back again. When he spoke he sounded like a different person. His voice was trembling.

"Boy, you trying to tell me I can't sell my good land, this corner I got here? I say I can. You trying to tell me I can't? Boy, I been here a long time. My wife is buried up there back of the house. Raised a family on this land. Just one daughter left with me now. But I know this place. Now you come in here telling me this place ain't good for nothing."

"I ain't said the place ain't good for nothing," Israel cut in, "but not for no gas station."

"I heard what you said. Was a time I wouldn't let a white man, let alone a black man, dispute my word, and I'm saying somebody going to buy my land, and don't you, nor you neither, dispute my word."

David said, "I won't dispute your word, Mr. Haywood. We both believe you can sell here. I reckon land around here sells for about three or four hundred dollars an acre."

"More. More than that, and I got upward of forty acres."

"But you don't want to sell out all of it. Just the corner?"

"That's right, maybe one, two acres here on the corner. That makes the store and the bins out back."

Israel said, "Reckon you want a good price for the one acre. Maybe much as a thousand dollars?"

The old man stood straight. He pointed his finger.

"Now I know you crazy," he said. "You know what them oil people, Standard and like that, pay for a corner? It's twenty thousand, thirty thousand, and sometimes more even, and you talk about one thousand! You must be crazy."

"Oil company ain't buying this corner, Mr. Haywood."

"Never mind, boy. Whosoever I sell it to, I ain't

selling my good corner for peanuts. I'm getting my price."

They did not stay much longer. A customer came in, a teen-age girl buying sugar and two cans of sardines. Israel observed that it would be dark soon and they'd better be getting home because Velvet would not want them to be late for dinner.

As they got in the car, Haywood called to them.

"You tell them gasoline people, Standard Oil and them, you tell them you know a good corner for a service station."

Ten

In the next few days, with Israel beside him, David drove over most of the county. He found no place that he liked more than the Haywood store.

In the far west end of the county they saw a vacant house on an eighty-acre farm. The whole farm was for sale. The large house could have been remodeled to serve as office and residence for a doctor, but the house could not be bought without the farm.

They went through the rich bottom lands of White Creek.

"You can see how the plantations took over the small farms," Israel said. "The white folks built theirselves mansion houses and they made quarters and a settlement for the black workers."

"Did the farm owners lose their land for debt?" David asked. "How did the whites get it?"

"No, there wasn't much lost for debt," Israel said. "Most and generally the whites bought the blacks out.

You know, they got ways. First there was a lot of high taxes. Then there was deals made."

"Deals? Like what?"

"You know, like promise of a good job for life and a house with free rent. And it was the money too, cash, more than most folks ever knew their land was worth. Some our folks is crazy about some money in the hand."

"Yes, I've seen things like that."

"You know, when they got the money some went off and bought another piece of land, but most of them pooped off their money on new cars and big-timing. It don't make sense."

David agreed that many things seem not to make sense. Yet he knew there were reasons underlying all the actions and reactions of people. As he went around the county he saw the homes of some rich white people and he saw those of poor whites, whose living standards were as low as those of poor blacks. Many of the black people were not living in poverty, but none of them seemed to be rich. They could be thought of as comfortably fixed.

At the senior high school, Principal Smith showed him through the buildings and introduced him to faculty members and to a few students he designated as outstanding. The facilities would compare favorably with those of a modern high school in other parts of the country, David thought. In contrast to most city schools, South Town High was spread out. The grounds covered several acres, including model fields of tobacco and cotton, and animal-raising projects, as well as athletic grounds and two gymnasiums.

A fleet of more than thirty huge school buses supplied transportation for students. Very few of them lived within walking distance.

Smith repeated his hope that Dr. Williams would come back and settle. "I've been thinking a lot about it since I met you," he said. "Your presence, just the fact that you were here, would be an inspiration to our young people. In spite of anything else it would prove something. And you know many white people are still locked into the old myths of racial differences. I hope you will come."

David said there were still some things to be arranged, but he hoped to have his affairs settled soon.

He knew he would have to have good relations with a hospital, and Boyd Memorial was most convenient. While he did not like Harold Boyd personally, he believed Dr. Boyd would cooperate. He planned to call on him again before leaving for New York. Things would work out.

Joyce Palmer telephoned.

At the Mannings' party Joyce had said, "I can't cope with the competition. Too many people around, I'll never get to know you in this crowd."

"Yes, and I do want to see you again," he answered, "to talk about the differences and all."

She told him she lived with a widow near the community college and they exchanged telephone numbers.

When she called him, it was to invite him to meet her at her campus office on Wednesday after her last class.

He had no trouble finding the college. It was about half a mile from old Route One. It was raining. The side road was paved but it was narrow. David knew from experience that it would be slippery, and he took the curves with care.

In the administration office the clerks were expecting him. One of them volunteered to escort him to Miss Palmer's office.

There could be no doubt that she was glad to see him.

"You know," she said, "you are the first outside visitor I've had here."

She was glad he had come because she was so hoping that he was going to settle in the area. She wanted to talk with him and tell him that the people needed him. He expected that they would sit in the privacy of her office, but she wanted to get away.

"We could go to my place," she said. She lived in Alberta, a town about five miles away, and she ate with the family, but it was so "unprivate."

"Isn't there some place around where we might go and have dinner?" he asked.

"I was hoping you would suggest that, but on one condition: You be my guest. I am a working woman and I'm on salary; I'm thoroughly liberated."

David said he could take care of the cost of the dinner, but at her insistence he complied.

He suggested the Holiday Inn just north of South Town. She offered to drive her car but David did not accept that. As she got into her rain gear he noticed that the shapeless outer garment did nothing to conceal her good looks. She was tall, not as tall as he was but tall enough for him not to feel like stooping to meet her. Her color was a rich brown, much darker and richer than the drab khaki-like coat and the hood which she pulled over her wavy black hair.

As they walked down the hall she stopped in another office to introduce him to the chairman of her department. "Dr. Williams is an M.D.," she told him, "and we hope he will be setting up practice near here."

As they got underway in the VW he said, "Now, look. I am David, or Dave for short. You dig?"

"I dig. And I'm Joyce. O.K.?"

They talked about the weather and the coming Easter vacation, his plans to return to New York at the end of the week and her plan to go to Atlanta to visit friends during that season.

Then she asked, "Did you like what you saw of us at the party last Saturday?"

"Yes, of course," David answered. "You know, the whole thing was so like a lot of other parties I've been to, with just a few differences."

"*Vive la différence!* And what were they?"

"Well, in the first place, there wasn't as much drinking of liquor."

"Score one for our side."

"And there was little or no dancing. If there had been, I would have danced with you."

"I'm not sure if that is one up or one down for our side."

"Other than that it was a good party—pleasant people, beautiful women, good food, and plenty of eggnog."

"With country corn liquor . . ."

"And a balmy evening in April."

"What did you think about our whites?"

"I'm not sure." David paused for a moment as he thought about the question. "They seemed to be all right, like they were wanting to be friendly, but I couldn't help wondering what they thought when our friend, the man Hart, came on with his Black Identity thing."

"Was that new to you? I've often heard such talk in mixed crowds up north. Sometimes the whites are on one side and sometimes on the other. One of my friends at Columbia was married to a white fellow who was an extreme militant. He often said he wished he were black."

"Yes, I've known some like that," David agreed.

"This fellow, Tom, insisted that his wife wear her hair natural and he tried to cultivate a bush for himself. He grew a beard and came out to parties wearing dashikis and robes. He read everything too, Du Bois, Fanon, Elijah Muhammad."

"I know what you mean." David described some of the whites he had known who seemed to want to identify with blacks. "Somehow," he concluded, "they never seemed to quite make it across the line. But the ones at the party were not like that. They seemed to want to be friendly and share their thoughts and experiences. They were quite sure of their relationships and confident in themselves."

"I think they were all right," Joyce said. "We have some at the college who are very unsure of their relationships, even with the few black people on faculty. And like you say, they lack confidence in themselves."

They talked about the possible differences between the approaches of southern white people, and they agreed that a man like John Smith, who admitted he had been fearful of contact with black people, was more honest than one who might claim to be without prejudice but actually have many negative emotions.

It was still raining, not hard but enough to keep the highway wet. At the crossroads the red clay lay in slippery patches. At each one David took it slow.

They came up a long hill and ahead lay level ground—but trouble was in sight. Several cars had stopped; most of the drivers had pulled to the soft shoulders.

On the right of the road a car lay upside-down. Its wheels were still turning in the air. Farther ahead another car was torn open along one side. In the roadway people were moving and calling to one another.

David turned the car off the pavement and braked. He was out the instant it stopped and he ran forward.

People were inside the car that was turned over. Some men were trying to help, but they were shouting at each other and no one seemed to be doing anything. Two bundles on the ground must have been people who had been thrown out of the other car. A child was screaming in hysteria and a woman was trying to quiet the child.

David ran and bent over one of the bundles, a woman. She was gasping for breath. Her left arm was twisted. Her sleeve was soaked with blood and the spot was enlarging. He knew he needed to see if there was heavy bleeding. He wished he had a pocket knife— without some tool he could not cut the cloth. She was lying on her right side. He pulled on the arm; from the way it came from the twisted position he guessed it was broken. He heard a man say, "Oh, God . . . Oh, God . . . why don't they send an ambulance!"

He straightened up to shout out, "Get in a car and go in town to call for help. They haven't heard about it yet."

The man turned away. David hoped he would act on the command.

Joyce was bending beside him. She helped to hold the victim's arm, and she helped to peel away the coat and another garment to show a gash in the white skin on the shoulder. Blood was coming from it in spurts.

"That's an artery, Joyce," David said. "This may be the worst of her injury. Come, we can check it. Kneel down there. See here: When I hold my hand down with pressure the bleeding stops. You've got to put your hand there. Yes . . . like that. Now hold. Now press *hard.* Hold so that the blood stops spurting. Good. You'll be dirty but you might save her life. Good girl!"

Joyce Palmer did not say anything. Her head was down. She was all attention. "Save her life" rang in her ears.

David went to the other victim lying on the road. The hysterical child was being carried away, its screams muffled in the arms of a woman.

The face David saw was that of a man of something more than middle age. The man lay on his back, quite calm, his arms stretched out, like one who waits in peace—or in death. His eyes were half open. The jaws were slack and the lips were parted. David felt for an artery at the neck. There was only a faint pulse. He pulled off his own raincoat with the jacket under it. He spread them over the injured man. Then he lay on the wet ground beside the man. He put his mouth over the victim's and started mouth-to-mouth respiration. Without lifting his head, he saw the feet of others. Between gasps of forcing air into the lungs of the victim he said, "Coats. . . . More coats. . . . Keep him warm. . . . More coats over him. . . . Coats under him. . . ."

Gradually he saw that others, probably people who had been driving, were trying to help. They were getting out of their coats. He well knew the victim might be beyond help, but he knew also that without help the man would surely be dead in a few minutes.

There was a gasp. Then David felt a pulse beat returning. He brought the man's arms across the body and with rhythmic movements caught the action of the man's chest with pressure-relax, pressure-relax.

"He's coming round," someone said above him.

Now he took time to look over at Joyce Palmer. It would not be good to cut off all blood from the arm for too long, but he thought it would not be too long yet. He had to disengage himself from the man he was working with.

"Mister," he said, speaking close to the man's ear. "Can you hear me?"

There was a feeble nod of the head.

"Listen, now," he went on. "You've been in an accident but you're going to be all right. Help is coming. Don't try to get up. Keep quiet. Just wait here."

The whine of an ambulance siren was in the air. David knew that there would be a lot of work for the ambulance crew whatever it might be. He did not know anything about the people in the car which was turned completely over. The ambulance people were near it.

A second ambulance was pulling into the area. It passed by the first ambulance and stopped on the road near David and the victim. A man came down from the front seat.

"I haven't examined this patient," David said, "but he wasn't breathing and he showed no pulse. I gave mouth-to-mouth respiration. He seems to be reviving."

"We'll get him on a stretcher and take him in. Can he help himself at all?"

"I don't know," David said, "he could have a back injury. Should be handled carefully."

The young man straightened and said, "I'll take charge, boy. You don't tell me how to handle a patient." He called to the driver, "Mack, bring a stretcher and get this man aboard it." Then, turning back to David, he said, "Now you get out of the way."

Someone in the crowd said, "That black boy might have saved the man's life. He sure knew what to do."

David said nothing. The stretcher arrived. It was put down beside the injured man. David reached out to bring it closer.

"Boy, you keep your hands off of the equipment. I'll have your ass in jail before night."

David looked up, without rising. He said in full voice and slowly, "I am David Andrew Williams, Doctor of Medicine, licensed in the state of New York and in the reciprocal states."

While the ambulance attendant looked his surprise someone in the crowd said, "The black man is a doctor."

"I didn't know," the young man said. He knelt beside David, and with the help of the driver the three men got the victim on the stretcher with a minimum of motion that would disturb his back.

"A woman over there has severe arterial bleeding," David said. "The lady with her has been applying pressure."

"Thanks, Doctor," the young man said as he moved away.

The first ambulance moved off. It took away the injured who had been trapped in the overturned car.

David watched as the ambulance attendant relieved Joyce of her duty. He spoke politely to her and thanked her.

Joyce was badly shaken by her experience. As she rose from her knees she looked ashy. David knew she was at the point of collapse now that the tension was released. She swayed and would have fallen. His arm went around her and her head bowed on his shoulder.

"You were great," he said. "You really did save that woman's life."

Joyce was trembling. A hand went up to clutch the collar of David's shirt. Blood, red raw blood, spread on the shirt. Joyce saw it and she screamed. And screamed again. Her eyes were wide with terror. She turned away and tried to run.

David caught her. He held her close and spoke softly into her ear. "It's all right. It's all right. I'm not hurt."

The screams stopped. Sobs came from her in gasps. One of the men who had helped brought David his raincoat and his jacket. With his handkerchief he tried to wipe the blood from Joyce's hand. There were splotches, too, on her clothes. His own clothes were damp and muddy.

The ambulance attendant came to them.

"Doctor," he said, "I'd be right glad if you would come in and help with the reports. . . . Boyd Memorial Hospital. You know where it is?"

"Yes," David replied. "I know."

They did not go to the restaurant for their own planned dinner party. David understood that Joyce would have to change her clothes, and his own were not what he would want them to be. When they got back to the car she asked him to return to the campus so she could get her own car. Then he drove behind her back up old Route One to the house where she lived.

Mrs. Short, the widow with whom Joyce lived, was all sympathy. While Joyce went upstairs to change her clothes Mrs. Short had David take off his shirt.

She said, "Only way to get blood out is to wash it in cold water while it's fresh, but I reckon the doctor knows that already."

David sat in the living room alone while she went to the kitchen. She was soon back, saying, "Now I put it to soak."

She started a conversation, wanting to know just who his people were and what church they attended.

"Miss Palmer told me you used to live near South Town."

Mrs. Short said she remembered Sister Williams from going to church conventions. Her church in Alberta was a brother-sister church to the Oak Grove Church in South Town. She soon went back to the kitchen. When she came out again the shirt was washed.

"The blood stains came out real good," she reported. Soon the shirt would be dry enough to be ironed.

Now Mrs. Short wanted the doctor to know that Miss Joyce Palmer was a mighty fine young woman. She was good as well as being smart book-wise. She had been at the college only about six months, but everybody knew she didn't fool around and that she held herself like a real lady.

When Joyce came down again she had changed her clothes. She was wearing a one-piece dress with short sleeves.

"I hope you feel better now," David said.

"I guess I do. The whole thing is still with me. I can't get over it. I'm still shaking. I can't go out again. I would be terrible company."

"Of course," David was quick to say, "I can understand. It was a difficult experience and you were in a crisis situation."

"I should be over it by now, though."

"No, not necessarily. While you were in it, while you were giving pressure, helping the injured woman, you were part of the scene. Once that was over and you had nothing more to give, you were pretty well drained. Then you suffered shock. Some women would have fainted at that point."

Mrs. Short agreed that she knew how it was. "Most and generally I can't stand the sight of blood," she said, "unlessen I'm doing something to help. I've had blood all over my hands and arms up to my elbows, but if I have to just watch somebody suffer I can't stand it. But you'll get over it, honey, and being a woman you will have more bad experiences and you will know."

David was feeling sorry to have to go. He was glad when Mrs. Short said, "What you need most of all is some food, something hot to settle your stomach. I've got some good bean soup on the stove and the rest of your dinner is ready."

"Well, I guess you are right, Mrs. Short," David said, "and I'll just go and let Miss Palmer have her dinner now."

"Oh, no," Mrs. Short said quickly, "you can't go now. You probably need something to eat same as she does. And it's all ready. Hope you don't mind eating in the kitchen."

It wasn't as David or Joyce had planned.

The kitchen was bright. David said it was just like home. The bean soup was hot. A ham shank had been boiled with string beans and potatoes.

David saw that the corn bread was not freshly cooked, and he remarked that his father had always said corn bread was better on the second day than when it was fresh.

He left early, saying that he really should go back

into town and check with the hospital. He promised to telephone and let Joyce know about the people—"especially," he concluded, "your patient."

He had all good feelings as he drove back to South Town.

He liked Joyce Palmer. When he first saw her she seemed to be an attractive girl, witty and pretty. She fitted well into the party crowd. On the campus she was different. Those with whom she worked recognized her as a competent professional. In the emergency she had shown courage, even toughness. In the simple home where she lived she had established a warm relationship with the widowed Mrs. Short.

She was more than a pretty girl. Joyce was an intelligent woman. He hoped she liked him. He wanted her to be a friend, and perhaps . . . but then, he admitted to himself, he hardly knew her.

At the hospital a nurse at the desk greeted him by name. She said that Dr. Boyd was not in but that Dr. Von Schilling was expecting him. She led the way to the office of the surgeon. She was a young black woman. Her starched cap sat high on her neatly cropped hair.

Dr. Von Schilling thanked Dr. Williams for coming in. He said the accident victims were very fortunate. He took his guest up to see them. Both were asleep under sedation. The other victims, those who had been brought in by the first ambulance, had not suffered serious injury. They had been examined and sent home.

The two doctors discussed the emergency treatment at the side of the road and the later treatment in the hospital. The prognosis for both patients was very good.

Back at the surgeon's office, seated at the desk, they checked drafts of the reports. David gave his address as Bellevue Hospital, New York City. He also gave Joyce Palmer's name and her address at the community college.

Dr. Von Schilling thanked Dr. Williams for his cooperation and said he certainly hoped he would be coming to the community as soon as his residency was completed.

"Our Dr. Boyd is young," he said, "and thoroughly provincial. I cannot share all his views."

"Yes, I've known Harold Boyd and his family for a long time," David answered. "I believe I understand him. As you say, he is young. I hope he will change because I'll have to depend on this hospital for specialized services, your work as surgeon, and the excellent facilities here, staff and equipment."

"No problem. No problem, I'm sure." Dr. Von Schilling lowered his voice and leaned forward to say, "There are many things on which he and I disagree, but I do what I think is best and in the end he accepts my judgment. You'll not have any serious trouble with him, and I believe you do understand him."

Eleven

David told the Crawfords that he would have to leave for New York on Saturday morning.

"I've made up my mind," he said. "I am coming back, only I wish I could know more about where I could get set up."

"Well, I think Old Man Haywood is asking too much for his place," Velvet said. "Talking about twenty thousand. His piece of land ain't no gold mine."

"Course he was talking about for a gas station," Israel said, "but I told him ain't nobody going to put a gas station on that corner."

"Didn't you tell him you thinking about buying it for yourself?" Junior asked David.

Israel said, "We thought we better hold that. Just sounding him out."

"Well, I 'clare," Velvet protested. "How come you didn't come on out and say what it was you was thinking? You men say that women hold back their real thinkings. I always say if you want to buy something you can say so, like I want to buy this place, I can pay you one hundred dollars or one thousand dollars or whatever you got in mind."

"Just ain't no way to do business, that's all," Israel said. "Women don't know how to do business."

"I do know the man got a right to know what folks is talking 'bout," Velvet said. "Like who it is talking about buying, and like how much he figuring he can pay."

"I guess you're right, Velvet, but like Israel said, we were just feeling him out. The truth is, twenty thousand is more than I could pay, but maybe I could swing half that much. My mother's going to sell the house in North Town, and she's willing to put the money in to help me get set up."

"But it will take a heap more than that to get the place fixed for office," Israel said.

Velvet added, "And for all the things a doctor needs—X rays and special kinds of tables and all."

"And desks and lab equipment and all kinds of cabinets," Junior said.

"Yes. It will take a pile, but the medical supply houses, they're willing to sell those things on credit. Those things don't come cheap, but doctors are expected to have high incomes even in their first years of practice."

"Maybe it wouldn't be like that here," Israel said, "but you know we got some savings, David. Velvet and me, we done talked it over. We could help."

"Well thanks, folks. I sure appreciate that, and I know that it wouldn't be for too long. I could sure pay you back."

They talked about possibilities and difficulties and hopes and fears. Finally they agreed that on the next morning David should go back to see Haywood. Both Velvet and Israel would go with him.

"And I'm going to do just like you said, Velvet. I'm going to put it straight to the old man, what I want, why I want it, how far I can go, and I'll make him an offer."

The next morning, before they left the house, Israel said to David, "You know how it is: Money talks." He handed David some money. "Take this thousand dollars in your hand. I'm loaning it to you. He liable to want to argue the price, like trading, and he won't take the first price, but you can deal with him. Let him see it. Give him all or part of it for earnest money."

David was surprised to know that Israel would have so much money on hand. He knew, however, that many people like the Crawfords did not trust banks and bankers. They often kept their money and their deeds and other valuable papers in locked metal boxes which they hid on the premises, in the house or in one of the barns. Sometimes the safes were buried.

At the store, Haywood went through the formalities of asking about the health of everybody—David, his mother, his sister—and how long his father had been dead. Then he asked Israel about Israel, Jr., and he asked Velvet about "all them pretty little gals." He spoke of the weather and crops and the season's outlook for tobacco and the hopes for good prices.

David had to bring the talk to business.

"Mr. Haywood, we want to talk to you some more about your place," David said as soon as he could get around the greetings.

"I got upwards of forty acres."

"It's only about the corner acre here. I told you I've been away studying to be a doctor. Well, I'm about ready to come back. I want to be a doctor right here. I figure I could start working right on this corner, make this store into an office. I'm thinking if you would sell it to me I could get started at my work and you could go on with the farming you want to do, taking up all the rest of the farm."

He did not give Haywood a chance to stop him.

"Now, I don't have a lot of money and I won't be making a whole lot of money when I start waiting on the people, but I'd appreciate it if we could come to an understanding. I've got to go to New York and get things together. I can come back after the first of July.

"Mr. Haywood, I can give you five thousand dollars

for one acre of land here on this corner with the store building on it."

Israel stood at one side. He was watching the old man's face. Velvet had moved away. She was looking at the shelves with their few cans and many paper-wrapped packages and the stacks of dusty books.

"Well, good God, boy." Haywood paused and looked around, looked out the door, looked at Israel and at Velvet and back at David. "Well, good God, boy, I been here on this corner a long time. I been a merchant right here seeing folks come and go, seeing your daddy and your mammy before you was born. Good God, boy. A man don't sell out his life like he sell a bag of flour. I got to set and think. Take me a few days to get it straight in my mind."

"It's a good offer, Mr. Haywood," David said. "I have to leave here tomorrow."

"You mean it's cash, all cash, no paper?"

"Yessir, Mr. Haywood. I mean cash. No paper."

"I got to set and think. Well, good God, boy. I got to set and think."

Mr. Haywood meant what he was saying. He turned away and went to the back of the counter and he sat on a stool, his hands folded in front of him like those of a child in school.

David stepped forward and counted out money, half spread, on the counter and concluded by saying, "I'm able to hand you five hundred dollars, that's ten per cent of my offer, five thousand dollars for the property."

Haywood looked at the money. He said nothing. David knew that this was not a poor man. People in the area used to say he still had the first dollar he ever took in at the store. Surely many more had gone to join the first.

"Not enough," he said finally. "You talking about paying for one acre of land, and maybe that's all right, but I got a store building on this property and that's worth another piece of money. Best I can do is five thousand for the land and plus five thousand for the store."

It was like Israel had said. The old man wanted to bargain, to offer and counter-offer, and hopefully come to a price. David wanted the place, and he believed Haywood wanted to sell. The best thing that could be said about the building was that it appeared to be sound. Before he was out of high school David had worked in a hardware store. Later he had spent summer vacation weeks working on construction jobs. He knew that with plywood paneling and with asphalt tiling on the floors the building could be well finished.

Haywood talked about the good construction of his building. He had been with the carpenters, watched them, seen that good lumber went into it, and he had added on the extra part in the back. "Probably stand right here for a hundred years," he said, "all oak beams and cypress two-by-fours. You can't hardly drive a nail in them."

David countered with probable cost of converting the building. ". . . And plumbing," he said, "I've got to put in plumbing, an electric pump for running water, and then a disposal system, septic tank or something like that. If the running water system and the plumbing were already here, I could see paying you more money."

Haywood laughed at the idea. "I been here on this corner nigh to forty years. Never had no plumbing and I ain't never had no trouble getting out to the privy. It ain't been that dark at night and it ain't been that cold in winter. Got a good well. Can bring in water by the bucketful. It ain't never run dry yet. I got to charge you for the store building as well as the land."

Israel did not take part in this conversation. He stayed in the background, acting as though he was not interested. He walked around the room looking at the scanty displays on shelves and at the cards tacked up with their advertising of cigarettes and automobiles and fancy perfumes and patent medicines. Just the same, David was aware that Israel and Velvet were listening to every word.

Finally Israel turned toward the two bargainers and he spoke. "How come you all don't try to get together?" he asked. "Mr. Haywood, everybody knows you want to sell the place, and David here, Dr. David

Williams, he wants to buy. I say you all ought to meet in the middle of the stream. David say five thousand, you say ten. Why can't both you all say seven, five? That's more than anybody else be paying, and it's the place that suits the doctor business."

The two men, old and white, young and black, eyed each other. Israel's words made sense. Haywood muttered something without agreeing. David took out his wallet and put more money on the counter.

"Them gas and oil people liable to be here any day and take this place over, but boy, I knew your pappy and your mammy and I be wishing you well, now you got your schooling and all, and that's the only reason I'm willing to make the sacrifice, so I settle for five thousand on the land and plus three thousand on the store, total eight thousand, all cash, pay on the barrelhead come July."

"I'll agree to that," David said, although he believed that if he had had more time to bargain, he could have gotten a better deal. "Here's eight hundred dollars earnest money, and you give me a receipt for this and everything'll be straight."

"I don't want your money now, boy." Haywood shook his head. He put his hands behind him and he stepped back. "My word is my bond. Everybody knows me. You just hold onto that and get the rest of the money to go along with it."

David tried to insist but he had to withdraw without

a paper. It was as though he really had something less than a deal.

As they rode back to Israel's house David felt that he had been defeated. He handed Israel the money and he thanked him.

"Wish I had something to bind the bargain," he said. "The way it stands he's not bound to sell me the place, and we don't have a firm price. He can go up if he wants to."

"Figure it this way, David," Israel said, "you ain't bound either. You change your mind, maybe you decide you don't want to be a country doctor . . . then you ain't out nothing. If a better place shows up for a better price, you can reach and get it. There's advantages both ways."

Velvet agreed. "You done all right," she said, "and you got just as much advantage as him. Can't tell what liable to happen 'tween now and July."

"Well, I'd like to be able to tell my mom what's happening. She'll be wanting to know, and when she gets here she'll run the house or however much there is to run."

"I'm glad to know that," Velvet said. "Nice to have your ma backing you up, putting some cash money and like that, but David, you a big boy now, you a man full grown. What you truly need is a wife, your own woman doing your housekeeping."

"Yes, I know," David laughed, "but there's nothing I can do about that just now. In the first place I can't ask anybody to come in now to help me get started. Let me get set up first . . . I've got nothing to offer."

"Well, sure 'nough," Israel agreed. "But he wouldn't want just any girl to marry. He got to have somebody special, maybe like that lady teacher at the community college."

"Her or somebody," Velvet said, "but a man full grown needs a wife in his house more than he needs a mother. You got to do something about that, David."

When they approached the house they saw a strange car parked on the side of the road. Two white men were waiting for them. As David drove into the driveway the visitors walked toward the front steps. The younger man carried a camera.

"We're looking for Dr. David Williams," the older man said. "We're from the paper." He gave his own name and that of the man with the camera.

They were doing a story about the accident. They asked for details and they wanted to take his picture. He answered their questions and told them about Joyce Palmer, without whom the woman probably would have died.

From the reporter he learned that the injured man was an insurance broker from Richmond. He and his wife were on their way back from Florida. The highway patrol thought that the two cars had met head-on. One or perhaps both of them had been skidding in the slick red mud. The woman had been thrown from the car. The man might or might not have gotten out under his own power. He himself did not know.

They were out of danger and they were asking to see the man who had saved their lives.

David thanked them for coming. He gave them the office telephone number for Joyce Palmer. They took his picture and left, saying that those folks sure were lucky.

"It's true?" Velvet asked. "You did sure 'nough save those people's lives? I bet they want to give you a reward."

"No, Velvet. It won't be like that. I couldn't take anything. It wouldn't be right. After all, what I did was really just a little first aid. It wasn't an operation, besides they didn't call me. They didn't come and ask for service. I just happened to come along. Anybody would have done the same thing."

"Anybody wouldn't know what to do," Israel said, and Velvet added, "Even that lady the teacher, I bet she wouldn't have known what to do to help the white lady if you didn't tell her."

"When you go see them in the hospital, you going take that teacher with you?"

"I won't be going to see the victims."

The others expressed their surprise. "Why?"

"There's nothing to see them about."

"David Williams, you may be a doctor and all but I'm lots older than you, and I want you to listen to me," Velvet said.

"He won't listen," Israel said. "He done made up his mind."

"Well, how about unmaking it?" Velvet demanded. "The man want eight thousand dollars for his corner. O.K., so you can handle that, but what about all the money it going to take to get started? Fixing it up to live in and to make it a doctor's office? What with furniture and plumbing and all, and all them things in a doctor's office. I bet they don't come cheap."

Israel agreed that the businessman would want to show his appreciation and that he truly owed a heavy debt for the saving of his life, but he also said he understood why David would not want to go to see him. He and Velvet argued about it. She said, "Could be David going to need a loan, and maybe if the man not rich even, he could know some banking people that could help."

"I tell you," Israel answered, "if David need some help he ain't got to go to no white man to get it. We see to that."

Later, Velvet wanted to know more about Joyce

Palmer. David told what he knew, but when Junior came in from school he gave a more elaborate description.

"She is truly what you call a fox," he said. "She came to our school and she spoke in assembly. If I ever do go to college I sure want to be in her class."

Twelve

When David returned to Bellevue on the Monday after Easter, he found he was assigned to the children's division.

"They should have told me before I went away," he said. "Then I could have been going over my notes and studying up. A man can forget about children when he works with adults over a long period."

"With you off and in the country you wouldn't have been studying about us up here anyway," one of his friends said. "I'll be going to Miami for my two weeks and I expect to sleep, sleep, sleep, just lie in the sun and sleep. I feel like I'll never catch up."

Dr. Kirkpatrick, director of residents in training, always emphasized the fact that general practitioners would use most of their time and their skills with children. He called David in for conference.

"Doctor, I'm glad to know," he said, "that you are

following through on your plan to return to South Town."

He said that he recognized the need for specialists—surgeons, heart men, gynecologists, and all the others—but family practice was also in its own way a specialty. A few years ago the field had been ignored by young medics. Now more of them, like Dr. Williams, were accepting it as their field of dedication.

"But I'd like to see more family-practice men going to the small towns. Perhaps the South, where you're going, needs them most, but lots of our rural areas right here in New York State are not properly served."

David told the director that he was hoping to set up in the country several miles from the town itself.

"Well, good! More power to you. What are the hospital facilities in the area?"

"There is a hospital in the town."

"How is it? Modern? Well equipped and staffed? Will you be helping them there?"

David thought it would be difficult to explain to this man from Minnesota the complexities of white-black relations in the South.

"Oh, it's modern, well equipped, and they have an excellent surgeon. There may be some problems, but I believe we will reach a good relationship. There are some personal elements. . . ."

"Personal?" Dr. Kirkpatrick did not understand.

"Well, for one thing, it's a memorial hospital. It's

new and it was built by the father of the young doctor who is chief of staff and everything."

"I see." The director was nodding. "I've known of such a situation. Never had to deal with it myself, but I know things can get sticky. Probably the father is chairman of the board and the board has little to say about how he runs his hospital."

David agreed.

"Anyway, Dr. Williams, I'm sure they will soon know what you can do and they'll be wanting you to help. I hope these last few weeks at Bellevue will be profitable. You know the sick child is often the product of a sick family. You'll have to treat the family as well as the child."

"I agree, sir," David answered, "and it's probably especially true about the people where I'll be working. I'll be living close to them, really in the country. I want to know them, and I want them to know me, and to trust me. I hope I'll be able to help them."

As Dr. Kirkpatrick rose to end the conference he wished Dr. Williams well, and he said that Bellevue would be ready and willing at any time to help with special problem cases.

On his new assignment David had little time to think of the problems he had left in South Town. He had cause to worry about Haywood and the fact that there was no real commitment regarding the sale of the property. He was, however, determined to return to the area and establish his practice somewhere in the county, preferably on a back road. Haywood's place seemed to be ideal.

His duties were not as pressing as when he had served in the children's division as an intern. From his comparatively lofty height as a resident he could see the system with better perspective. He recognized that there was order and direction where he had thought there was erratic movement and confusion.

After the first week he was able almost to forget the problems in Pocahontas County. The pressures were not so great but he was kept busy. There were so many things for him to learn. When he was free, and not too tired or sleepy, he went to the library.

Bellevue Hospital provided pleasant lounges for each level of staff members. Interns, residents, and nurses had their own rooms furnished with sofas and low tables and easy chairs grouped around color television sets. Coffee and snacks were always available. It was presumed that staff members would go to their lounges for relaxation and conversation.

As intern and as resident, David had found little time for use of lounges.

The library was something different. The library was not designed for relaxation but it did have social usage. Lines of occupation were not recognized in the library. It was a place where interns and residents and nurses could and did enter into conversation with each other and sometimes with the highest officers of the hospital administration.

Conversations would be informal. Often they were quite casual. They might deal with questions of "How long have you been here?" and "What are you doing now?" and "Where are you going?"

The training year for interns and residents at Bellevue runs from the first day of July to the last of June. On the last day of their year, interns move out. They become resident doctors at Bellevue or they go to other hospitals where they will be in residence for two years or more. On the same day, doctors who are finishing their residencies take their departure. There are no graduation ceremonies. Some who are leaving will gather for parties. There are no official social activities. Inevitably there is a slowing up of hospital functions.

As the month of June drew to a close, David shared questions and answers in the library. Few showed surprise when they learned that he was going to start his work in the southern countryside. To those who did question his choice he said, "I was born there."

The last day of June was a Sunday. He was invited to two parties. One was on Saturday night at the apartment of a married doctor who was completing three years of residency. He was white. They were not close friends, but they had shared some duties at Bellevue. David knew the doctor's wife, who was also a doctor. The other party was to be a dinner on Sunday evening at a downtown hotel. The honored guest was a black doctor who was finishing two years of residence. He and David hardly knew each other. David thought he was being invited only because he was a "brother." He declined with thanks.

He went to the Saturday night party. The food was good and there were drinks. Conversations were almost entirely professional. Doctors and nurses and technicians and social workers seemed to find it difficult to forget their patients. Perhaps, he reasoned, that was as it should be.

On Sunday morning he telephoned to his mother in North Town.

"You are going to come home for a little rest, aren't you?" she asked.

"Sorry, Mamma. I just can't make it," he said, explaining that he needed to get back to South Town as soon as possible. "I've got to get that deal started with Haywood, and everything else. I'll rest later."

He walked through the halls of Bellevue for the last time. In the men's surgery ward he hoped to speak to Nurse Jenkins—Jenks, as she had invited him to call her. She had helped him when he was a new intern, awkward, confused, and perhaps frightened. Jenks was not there. Two other nurses on the ward remembered him. They wished him well.

There were few others he wanted to see. He had said

good-bye to Dr. Kirkpatrick when they met for conference after Easter. He had come to appreciate two or three of the orderlies. But the best of those young men did not work on Sundays.

He had bought a second-hand station wagon, and in the afternoon he brought it around to the back parking lot. In it he stowed his books and a few precious instruments, his clothes, most of them woefully out of style, and all his possessions from his room. Someone else would be moving in on Monday morning.

He would like to have gotten on the road immediately, but there was some work to be done on the car.

Then he wished he had accepted the dinner invitation, but it was too late.

He spent the night in a motel room. He slept fitfully, wondering why in three years at Bellevue he had made no close friends in the great city of New York.

Thirteen

It was the third day of July when Dr. David Williams came again down old Route One to South Town. In the station wagon he had practically everything he owned.

It was hot. He had been driving most of the day. He had started the trip tired after rearranging his affairs in New York.

He thought about going around to Brown's Cafe. He would like to see Al Brown. But on this day Al would be very busy. Besides, he wanted to get out to the Crawford place. Israel would have the late news. He had written to let them know he would be coming.

It took only a few minutes to pass through the town. Certainly it looked very different from the way it had looked when he lived there, but he had a warm feeling that he was actually coming home. It was a beginning and an end, the beginning of a new life as a medical doctor, actually on his own. He would be without the kind of supervision he had gotten used to as an intern and as a resident doctor in the hospital. He would be on his own, responsible, making diagnoses that were, hopefully, correct, but at times inevitably incorrect. He would have to arrange his business affairs, secure the location, equip the office, make arrangements for some help, and set up a system of records.

Oh, yes, there was a lot to do in this beginning of a new life.

And it was the end. The end of being away, off in school, off with his parents, working part-time, working hard through summers, making it at football, and giving that up because it was too hard to study and work and play football.

It was the end of what could have been a start in hardware business, or life as a carpenter, a builder, a contractor.

It was the end of many things, and it was the beginning.

He saw the Crawford house ahead of him. It had been newly painted and it seemed larger than he remembered it. He took his foot off the gas and braked easily to make the turn from the highway into the driveway. Velvet's flower garden was rich with hollyhocks, zinnias, and tall larkspurs.

Junior's dog, old Woolford, started barking. David bore down on the horn and he saw Junior come running out the front door, banging the screen and running and jumping from the porch without using the steps.

Israel came around from the back of the house, shouting his welcome. "Come on in the house, man! Give the buggy a rest. Come on in the house!"

Junior slapped David on the back, and David grabbed the boy in a bear hug.

When Israel got to him there was more hugging and back pounding. "What kept you so long? We been looking for you all day."

They told him that Velvet had gone over to the Manning place to pick up the girls. They had been having some kind of rehearsal.

"But your room ready for you," Israel said.

"It's real right ready," Junior said. "Just wait 'til you see it."

Junior admired the station wagon. It was not a late model, but it looked respectable and David had bought it at a good price.

"Might as well start toting in," Israel said. "Look like you got right much of a good load."

They loaded up, talking, Junior anxious to help.

As they went up the wide steps David recognized a change. The house had been widened. The porch was extended to the left, and this was the way that Israel led.

"Come on in the house, man," he said again as he opened a door. David followed and found himself in a large room smelling of new wood and paint. The floor was not carpeted. It was bare but swept clean.

"Wait 'til you see it all," Junior said behind him. He rushed in and went beyond where a hall went through to the back. David followed and saw a door opening into a room in which a bed was made up with a patchwork quilt. Beyond the bedroom door a bathroom opened with shiny new fittings, glistening white and chrome, and a linoleum tile floor.

"But you've practically built another house, Israel. And so fast. It wasn't started when I was here before."

Israel was happy. Junior kept showing features. The shower bath, the kitchen sink with handles for hot and cold but only one swivel spout. A new dinette set of chrome and plastic, a brand-new electric refrigerator, and a small electric range.

David hardly knew what to say. Israel and Israel, Jr., hardly knew when to stop.

"You know, David," Israel said, "it wasn't just for you, but our young ones are getting up, and we got plenty of them. The house your folks sold us was just fine when we weren't so many. Now we got a fistful of young folks and they getting underfoot. Velvet figured a long time ago on making it bigger, and with you coming back, well, we just figured this was the time to do what we going to do. Why wait?"

David was quick to admit that a room was very useful. In the spring he had felt he was putting others to inconvenience. They said the girls liked sleeping at their grandmother's. Now they had made an apartment. He was grateful to them, and he told them so.

They heard Velvet's car coming into the driveway, and then she and the girls were coming up the steps and into the room. They swarmed over and around David. They kissed him and held to him.

"We didn't try to put furnitures in this room," Velvet said. "Figured you'd want to pick that out yourself."

"Well, I don't need much, you know," David answered. "Really just a place to sleep for a while."

"Oh, no," one of the girls said, "you got to stay here. We're not going to let you move away."

And Israel added, "Can't say how long it might be, but it'll take a while." The family was planning to have him for a long time. "Can't tell about Old Man Haywood. He liable to want to talk some trash, but you ain't bound to put up with no stuff. If shove-come-push you can just stay right here. We can add on if we have to, and we can put up the sign out there, Dr. David Williams."

"That's right," Velvet said.

"No. No." Junior was shouting, waving his arms. "No. Here's how it goes: 'David Andrew Williams, M.D. Specialist in Everything.' "

"That'd be neat!" one of the girls said, screaming a little.

They told him that Haywood had said very little about David's offer. For a few days after David's visit the old man had been busy. He had closed the store and gone into town. One time he asked Israel if "that Williams boy" truly meant to do business.

Later, as they sat at dinner, David outlined his plans.

His mother had a sale for the home in North Town. She would be ready to come later in the summer.

"And what about Betty Jane?" Velvet asked.

"Of course school is out for the summer and Betty Jane will not be teaching. She's staying with Mamma for a few weeks. Maybe she'll come down for a visit."

"Sure would like to see her," Velvet said. "Just think—she was about the age of Angie here when you folks left, and she's never been back to look at us."

"Yes, and Uncle Dave was my age when he left here," Junior added.

"O.K., Big Boy," Angie said, laughing, "it's time you and me was moving out—Let's go—" Junior raised his hand in a mock threat, but everybody knew it was all in fun.

"After we get a deal completed with Haywood," David said, "we'll have to get with some builders to see about fixing up the place."

"You mean *if*," Israel said. "You mean *if* you get a deal. I'm thinking the man don't really plan to sell out, and if he do sell he will want to take a arm and a leg and lots more money than the place is worth. You'll see."

Velvet said again that what Haywood would do wasn't to be worried about, because they could sure set up Dr. Williams' office right there. It could be arranged permanently too.

Junior and the girls wanted to know about David's last few weeks in the hospital.

"I bet some of your patients were sorry to see you leave," Angie said.

David tried to make them all understand that in a large establishment like Bellevue Hospital the patients had little chance to know much about the doctors who served them. There were so many patients and so many doctors.

"I guess it's a production-line kind of thing," Junior volunteered. "Like a factory or a super service station."

David admitted that sometimes it looked like that.

"Still," he said solemnly, "I think that most of the doctors I worked with never could forget that the patients were real people, each one a separate personality, each with a bundle of different problems, a lot more problems than the disease or the damages in their bodies. I wouldn't say it was like a machine setup.

"And the doctors themselves, each one a different person, and very different from each other one."

"Were many of them black?" Junior asked.

"No. Very few were black, but that's not what I mean about them being different. Maybe it's part of it. Some of the guys in school were very smart, some of them were really great brains."

"I bet you were," Angie said.

David laughed. "No, you're wrong," he said. "I wasn't so smart. I never was anything extra in school. I had to dig. Some of my friends read it once and remembered. I was never like that. My chemistry and later my pharmacology, I had to memorize that stuff, sometimes walking the floor with a book in my hand to keep awake."

"Didn't you ever want to drop out?" Junior asked.

"I never stopped to think too much about it. Dropping out was giving up. There were problems in staying with it, in hanging in there, but there were more problems in giving up."

They were all silent, waiting for David to go on.

"I guess I learned some things in playing football, and through it all there was my dad. He never pushed me. He never told me what I had to do or that I had to do anything. He let me make up my own mind, but he made me know that he was there.

"One time, when I was talking about how much it would cost to go through med school, he said, 'Well, if it'll cost more I guess it's worth more,' and then he said, 'I don't know how much it will take or how much I can do for you, but I'll do all I can.' "

Israel said, "Your daddy was a good man."

"And your ma was a strong woman," Velvet said.

"That I always knew."

"You're both right." David looked at them with a feeling of thankfulness. "One thing I wish: I wish I could have seen Pa after they gave me my degree from med school. He was there with Ma when they gave me my bachelor's degree from the State College but he was failing even then. If he could see me now, right here, back in South Town, and ready."

Velvet said, "David, for true, I know your daddy can see you right now. I just know it. I can feel it."

"Oh, Mom," little Ruthie said.

"Just old-fashioned superstition," Junior said.

"No, Junior." David spoke quickly. "It isn't 'just old-fashioned superstition.' It's a part of the latest scientific research. . . . Someday, soon maybe, we will know more about it. It is like the old song says: 'We will understand it better by and by.' It is not all superstition."

Fourteen

It was not easy to reach an agreement with Haywood, who had a good thing and knew it.

David thought they should go early in the morning, but Israel advised waiting until the afternoon. Haywood would not close for the holiday. In fact, he would be extra busy.

"Let him do what he got to do and then get tired," Israel said. "That way he don't have the strength to hold you off."

There was truth in the philosophy. David had read that people were apt to yield to pressure when they were tired. Tests had shown that people, especially older people, had definitely less sales resistance in the afternoon.

Although they did not go out, the house was busy from early morning. In the town a parade would pass along Main Street. The mayor would preside at ceremonies at the city hall. A visiting congressman was

going to make a speech. Some people around knew
that their Dr. Williams was expected back. They had
seen the framing and construction of the addition to
the Crawford place.

So they dropped in.

Velvet had cold drinks and cake and ice cream for
all comers. They admired the addition to the Crawford
house. Most of them thought Dr. Williams would be
opening his office there. No one in the family said it
would not be like that—no one, indeed, could be sure.

In the early afternoon David thought they should be
going. "I don't like to wait too long," he said. "Suppose
the old man likes to take a nap in the afternoon."

"That he do, but he just sits around in the store."

Israel went on to say that Haywood's friends, the old
cronies who liked to sit with him, would go to their
own homes for the midday meal. Then they would
sleep in the afternoon.

Junior wanted to go with David and Israel, but
Israel said, "This is business for men."

Haywood was not in a good mood. He responded
with little more than a grunt when David said he came
to talk business.

"Any time you're ready I'll be ready," David said.
"Maybe we ought to get your lawyer to draw up a
deed, and we'll need to get the surveyor to mark it off."

Haywood grunted again. He did not look at his
visitors. He twisted to look through the window far to

the back, where his house sat up on a rise. The wide branches of a great oak hovered over it. His daughter, Charlotte, sat in the porch swing, just swinging.

"Maybe we could meet in town, maybe at your lawyer's?" David said.

Haywood grunted again. Then he looked, not at David but at Israel, as he said, "How much you all figure to pay for my property?"

"When I was here before, we agreed on the price," David said. "Total eight thousand dollars, going three thousand for the store and five thousand for one acre of land."

"One acre of land?" Haywood turned toward David.

He was showing anger. It looked as though he were insulted. "I ain't selling no one acre of land. If I sell, I sell all my good land together. You think I'm going set up on that porch and watch somebody else take advantage of me and my heirs? It ain't going be like that. If I sell I'm going to get out of this Godforsaken country and go on back to South Carolina and live like a white man. If anybody want to buy my farm he can talk business, but I ain't interested in selling no one acre."

"But, Mr. Haywood"—David was trying to get in a word—"Mr. Haywood, you said you would sell for eight thousand. And you said, too, your word was good as your bond . . . and I thought . . ."

"Boy, you ain't got to tell me what I said. I know what I said. I never said I would sell. I said I'd think about it. And now I done thought . . . and I'm telling you and anybody else want to hear it, I'm telling you all I ain't selling nothing 'less I sell all, 'cause I'll be getting out."

Israel had said nothing, standing back, just listening. David was glad to know that he was there. Now he spoke. "Mr. Haywood, suppose somebody was going to buy you out, how much you be asking?"

Haywood grunted again. But he looked like he was pleased to talk a sale. "I figure if the one acre is worth five thousand, the forty acres ought to sell for two hundred thousand, but I be willing to make a good bargain price. I be willing to cut that way down, make it fifty thousand." He held up his hand as Israel started to answer, and he added, "Only reason I do that, I figure me and Charlotte can live on that for a spell with what few pennies I got saved. . . . And to sweeten the bargain I throw in the buildings—the store, the house, everything—lock, stock, and barrel, like the man say."

David turned and started for the door. "Let's go," he said as he passed Israel, who turned and followed David to the car.

Neither spoke as David drove the car on the road and headed back down the hill.

David was thinking as he drove that perhaps fifty

thousand dollars was not too much for the place. It was just an impossible price for him. He wanted the corner. The store building could serve his purpose very well. The structure was sound. The floors were level and the walls were plumb. For what he wanted to do it was better than anything Israel might arrange at his house.

He said nothing all the way home. Israel knew David was deep in thought and he kept his silence.

As they approached the Crawford place they saw that the cars of visitors were there. Israel said, "Let's don't stop now, David. I want to talk to you. Let's drive on by."

David had been slowing for the turn. He pressed down on the accelerator and went by the house, hoping that no one there recognized him.

He said nothing for another mile. The new high school sat high on the side of the road, closed now for the summer. Its red brick walls looked like they were enjoying a well-deserved rest. For nine months students from all over the east end of the county poured from buses every school-day morning. They filled the classrooms and halls to overflowing. Now there was no action. The flag was not flying from the pole. The halyard hung limp.

David got off the highway and drove up the incline into the parking lot and stopped the car.

"So what do you think?" he asked as he turned toward Israel.

"I think you want that place right bad," Israel replied. "Course me and Velvet was thinking maybe we could get you to settle down on our place. We sure would like to work something out . . . and we could do it easy."

"That would be good of you," David said, "but it would sort of kill your place as a home for your family."

"The family would like that, and besides, everybody would know just where you was at. It would be like you come back home. And they'd be proud of you."

"Yes, I know, Israel." David was shaking his head. "But I don't think I would like it. It would be a good business location. Everybody driving by on Route One could be pointing to it. They would think of it as a kind of hospital. It wouldn't be the Crawford place. Then they'd come to compare it with the Boyd Memorial Hospital and pretty soon they would be calling it 'the black hospital.' It would be like we were trying to do something and we couldn't bring it off."

"David, I didn't say this before"—Israel put his hand on David's arm—"I don't boast about it, you know, but David, fact is I got right smart money in land what I own free and clear. And that money ain't doing me too much good. Maybe a black hospital would be good to have in South Town. Folks wouldn't have to go to Boyd then. Yessir, I got money, and there's some more around here who could put up money. It ain't like it used to be.

"Listen, David, me and Velvet done talked this all out. She sees it same as me. That Dr. Boyd, he's like his daddy always was. He lets our people into the hospital but he treats them like he was handing down something that folks ought to lick his hand for doing, like they was dogs. I hope to God that neither me nor none of mine ever has to go to his hospital."

"Yes, Israel. There's a lot in what you say."

"And besides me and Velvet there's lots more around here say the same."

"But there's another way to look at it, Israel. Consider this: South Town does not need two hospitals. There aren't enough people in this area, black and white together."

Israel protested. "Even if ours wasn't so big," he said, "we could sure use it."

"But any hospital, large or small, ought to be the best possible. That much I have learned. Instead of trying to make another hospital, just for black people, we ought to be trying to make the Boyd Memorial a place for everybody, black and white."

"They won't do it," Israel said, shaking his head. "They won't never do it."

David had to laugh. "Did I tell you the first time I went into the hospital Harold Boyd offered me a job on his staff? At least he was thinking about integrating."

"I didn't know that. And you told him no?"

"I told him I wanted a small general practice, out of town, really in the country, but for some of my patients I'd be using Boyd Memorial. I know they've got good equipment there. They've got a good surgeon, and they do have the contacts with the capital and with the large V.A. hospital and those places where specialized work is done."

"You really believe Dr. Harold Boyd will cooperate with you and give full service to black folks?"

"In time, yes."

"But that's it, now! How long it going to take?"

"You can't tell. Things are moving fast." David turned his head and looked at the high school. "Maybe they're moving faster in the South than in the North, but anyway we can't turn back to building up more segregation."

"David, you been away from here, and you got your schooling and now you come back and I not so sure I understand what you're saying, but . . . but . . . I figure you ought to know more than me. I grant you that."

"You know how it was with the public schools?" David asked with the sweep of his arm. "When there were two sets of schools all the schools were bad, poorly equipped, inadequate. Schools for whites were poor enough and schools for blacks were worse. Now, with one system, all the schools are better, and black and white kids get the benefit. People have to learn to work together, to live together, and to be sick or well together. The big thing is that people can learn. That's how it will be with one good hospital and some general practitioners out and around the county."

Israel was nodding his head. "You could be right," he said. "I remember how folks said the schools couldn't be brought together. Black folks said it well as whites."

"And my office and the hospital business is going to work out, somewhere, somehow. It's too late to turn back."

"Yes. Too late to turn back."

They both stopped talking. They sat and thought. David was wondering if they could find another location, and he was wondering how or if he could arrange a mortgage deal and purchase the property.

Israel broke the silence. "David," he said, "tell me. You still think you want to set up at Old Man Haywood's place?"

"Yes. That's it."

"Then that's how it's going to be. We work it out."

"And you know," David said as he turned the key in the switch and the motor began to hum, "you know when I was in high school I worked part-time in a hardware store. That was a good part of my education. Then in college I worked summers in building construction. I joined the union. I know how to fix up a place."

"You a carpenter, David?"

"Not a finish carpenter," David admitted, "but I do know how to frame and how to use plywood panels. I know how to do electric wiring and plumbing. With a little help we can make a fine layout for a doctor."

"Sure 'nough!" Israel was pleased. "And I bet you can do more than old Mr. Liggett, who put those extra rooms at my place. He can't figure out nothing on paper but he sure is a good stick carpenter."

"A stick carpenter?" David asked.

"Don't you know what a stick carpenter is? He can't take no ruler to see how many feet and how many inches something is. He takes a stick. He lay it out. He says the thing is so many sticks and this much over. But it works."

"Oh yes, I remember." Now David was pleased. "I bet your Mr. Liggett could give a lot of good work fixing up. He sure made your place nice."

David could not see how, even with Israel's help, he could afford to buy the Haywood property at fifty thousand dollars. He had thought that Haywood's price of eight thousand dollars, plus the cost of rebuilding, would take about all that his mother would be able to provide. Israel's offer was encouraging, but David knew that Israel's resources were limited.

His biggest expenses would be for furniture, instruments, examining tables, X-ray machines, and other office equipment, and possibly an ambulance. These things, he believed, could be bought on credit. Suppliers were anxious to sell and doctors were good credit risks.

Salesmen had called on him. He and other young doctors at Bellevue had been given elaborate catalogues. Suppliers had entertained them at their showrooms. He had already made a tentative list of the items he would need.

He had been told not to worry about the prices or the cost. "What is best for your patients is cheapest for you," the suppliers had said.

That evening at the Crawfords', they sat on the porch again. David and Israel were seated on the top step. Velvet was in the swing. Junior and the girls were romping in the yard with half a dozen other young folk. They had some firecrackers and sky rockets and sparklers.

It was the first chance for Israel and Velvet to talk.

He told her about the visit to Old Man Haywood and about the conversation up on the schoolhouse hill.

"And I told David," Israel concluded, "that you and me both truly want him to have that place and we going back him up getting it."

"You're right, Israel," Velvet said, "you're sure right. We going back him up getting it. I don't rightly see how, just now, but we going work it out. That we will, God helping us. That we will."

Fifteen

Velvet's words expressed what all of them were thinking: "We going work it out, God helping us."

They talked about ways and means.

They agreed they did not want to seek the help of Mr. Boyd. As Israel had told David earlier, the man had a part in practically every real estate deal in the county. He collected commissions on most sales. He established prices. He gave approval—or withheld it—on each mortgage application that went through the bank.

David believed that Mr. Boyd, like his son Dr. Boyd, would consider David, the black Dr. Williams, an intruder and a threat.

Israel was willing to draw on his savings, possibly to borrow on land he owned, to help out. David said he really did not want anyone to borrow, to go into debt in order to help.

"Another thing," Israel said, "we got plenty people

around who got money laid by, same as me, and I
know they could put up two, three, maybe five
thousand dollars, pool their money. That's what it
would take."

David was less confident. Velvet thought such a
thing would not happen.

"David would be leaning on a bent twig," she said,
"if he depended on any one of these folks that got
maybe a little laid by. If they got it laid by they ain't
about to turn it loose, not for David, not for you, Israel,
or for nobody else, 'less it be a family need."

"The Browns, Mrs. Brown and Al, they got money,"
Israel said, "and then look at John Manning, I bet he
can raise much as me any time he wanted. Then
there's Skipwith and the Mayfields up to Boydton, and
those folks, some kind of cousins of yours, the Bowers,
in Chase City. All of them doing all right. They got
fine houses. Bet they got plenty laid by."

Velvet only grunted, or humphed, at each family
named.

"Fine houses," she said. "Fine cars. Fine clothes.
How you figure they going be laying up savings?"

"They got to be," Israel said.

"Tell you what I'm thinking," David said. "Israel,
you may be right. Anyway, Al Brown and his family
have been in business in South Town for a long time.
They must have made some deals. Then, like you say,
there's John Manning. He did a lot of building. He

must know something about financing. Maybe we ought to go see them. Maybe they would have some ideas."

Al Brown and John Manning did have ideas, or it might be said that they both had the same idea.

"Best thing for you to do is to talk to Dr. Hart over in Chase City," John Manning said. "You met him here at the party. Remember the right black man with the beard who wanted to start an argument with the whites? Well, he's a professor up at State College, teaches business. He talks a lot about race, but he's smart and he's not afraid of anybody, especially he's not afraid of white folks, like old man Haywood or Mr. Boyd, or, I reckon, the president of the United States. He would say, 'He's just another man.' "

Al Brown was even more hearty in his recommendation. "Dr. Hart teaches economics and business administration," Al said. "He really is a brain. He's a lawyer, admitted to the bar in this state. But he prefers teaching because he says business training is what our people need. They say he can really make his students understand principles of business, and financing, and contracts, and real estate and all that."

Brown got on the telephone. He found Hart at home and told him something about David's problems. Hart offered to drive over to the Crawford place on that same afternoon. He would have to go back to State

College at the beginning of the next week for summer-session classes.

When Hart joined David and Israel that afternoon, there was no talk of race. No one spoke the word "black" or its opposite, the word "white." There was no talk of courage or of fighting.

Hart was all business as they sat at a table in the new section of the Crawford house. Velvet did not join the men. She stayed in the swing on the porch.

Hart took a pad of ruled yellow paper from a briefcase and laid it on the table before him. He listened without speaking while David told him the story of negotiations with the storekeeper. When the final price of fifty thousand dollars was mentioned, he started making notes.

Then he started asking questions: What was the amount of money that Dr. Williams could receive from his mother? David gave an answer, using the term "about."

"Not 'about,' Dr. Williams," he said. "We must only count on the amount that you know your mother can send you by bank draft now."

David gave a figure.

"And from contemplated or expected sale of the house, do you know how much that will net?"

David admitted he did not know. He could not be sure what the mortgage balance was or what the selling expenses might be. His mother had told him the price at which the property was being sold, so he offered an estimate. Hart reduced the estimate by two thousand dollars and said that selling costs, points, brokerage, always came to much more than sellers expected.

Then he asked if there were any other assets, and Israel said he was ready to put up his money to help David get the place. The amount he quoted was more than David had expected.

"Is that amount immediately available—savings account or negotiable bonds—Mr. Crawford?"

"That's in my savings account. I ain't got no bonds, but I got more land, free and clear. I can always borrow on that."

Again David objected, and Hart agreed that Mr. Crawford should not borrow in order to lend. Israel fell quiet, but he looked as though he were hurt.

"So, Mr. Crawford, you can lend this amount, at say, eight per cent interest?"

"Oh, no. No, sir. I couldn't take no interest. You don't know how much David's family has meant to me."

Hart listened without change of expression. Then he said, "Mr. Crawford, I will not allow my client to borrow money from anyone without paying interest."

"But he's my friend," Israel insisted.

"Yes. So let's keep it that way," Hart answered.

Hart asked if Dr. Williams was sure that he wanted the place at the offered price.

Receiving a positive answer, he said, "I believe I can help you. We'll think in terms of fifty thousand dollars and an amount of five thousand within the next ten or fifteen days. After that we will see, hopefully within the range that you have given me. I will ask you not to have any contact with the seller or any of his agents. Refer all questions to me. All questions, from the seller and from any of your friends. My fee will be twenty-five hundred dollars, payable at closing."

"But . . . but"—Israel rose from his chair with his question—"but suppose the deal don't go through. What then?"

"It is my responsibility, Mr. Crawford, to see that the deal does go through. If peradventure it did not go through, my client would owe me nothing."

David asked, "Are you going up now to see Mr. Haywood?"

"No, Doctor, I'll see him in time. You have my number at my home. Messages can be left there, and I have your number here. So we will keep in touch."

Hart did not linger. He rose and left.

He tipped his hat with a flourish as he said good-bye to Velvet in the swing.

Sixteen

There was little for Dr. Williams to do for a while in Pocahontas County. He hoped, desperately hoped, that Dr. Hart would be able to bring about the purchase of the Haywood place. He could see there was no point in quizzing the man who would be serving as his agent.

"It's his specialty," he said to Israel and Velvet. "When a patient puts himself under treatment by a doctor, he should rely on the doctor as a specialist to do that which is best. If a man feels he can prescribe the medicine and treat himself, he doesn't need a doctor."

Velvet said, "You right, David, I believe that little old man do know what he's doing."

"I sure would like to be getting ready, though," he added. "I'd like to get out there and take some measurements, lay out some plans, maybe see what we're going to need—if we get the place."

Going back to Haywood's with a tape line would bring up more questions.

There were a few matters which demanded attention. He would have to go to the capital to see about his license to practice in the state. It would mean a visit to the office of the State Board of Medical Examiners.

"Will you have to take an examination?" Junior asked.

"No, hardly," he answered. "But in each state the board holds examinations for the year's med school graduates. They have a whole battery of tests in various fields."

"Are they tough?" Junior asked. "I mean, are the tests harder than the ones you had to pass in school?"

"Usually not. Still, they can be tricky, and sometimes a man, or a woman—lots of women are taking medicine now, you know—sometimes a person goes in to take the state board and fails it."

"Gosh, they must be dumb. Else the tests must be awful hard."

"Well, some folks tighten up every time they take an important exam. Then sometimes a person can be sick, have the flu or something, and go in and sit for it anyway. It's given only once a year. That happens."

"Now you got your license for New York," Velvet said, "what you got to do to get a license for this state?"

"They have a system; it's called reciprocity," David answered. "When the med school graduates file to take the state board, each one lists any other states where he might want to practice. So the board in New York notified the state board here that I was taking the exam. This state, if it wanted to, could have sent some special questions to New York to be added to the New York examinations. Later the New York board reported my grades to this state. If there had been any subjects that I did badly in or if the board here thinks the particular test didn't cover enough ground, then the state board here could still make me sit for more testing before giving me a license. That's not likely to happen, because everybody knows the New York board is one of the toughest in the country."

"Oh, I know you won't have any trouble"—Junior was proud of his Uncle David—"you got stuff for them."

Junior volunteered to drive.

On Sunday David telephoned to his mother in North Town. He gave her details of his plans. She told him that the house sale was to be completed by the first of August and she told him how much money she would have after all the selling expenses. She promised to draw from her savings account immediately and send him a check.

With Junior driving, David left after breakfast on Monday morning for the capital. They had no difficulty in locating the center of state affairs, a two-block square whose lawns and heavy shade trees were dominated by a marble-columned building with a high dome. State buildings of modern design faced the square. In one of these were the offices of the Board of Medical Examiners. Junior said he would park the car and wait.

When he stepped off the elevator on the tenth floor, David was wearing a seersucker jacket and a tie. He wanted to look professional. In the lobby, no one was at the desk marked "Information," but a wide door was open beyond the desk. David could see a larger room with filing cabinets. Some staff people were gathered there. A middle-aged man lolled back in an armchair at a wide desk. A young woman sat on the desk, her long legs dangling. Two men stood nearby. One man held a paper cup in his hand. Other paper cups were on the desk. They looked toward him when he entered, but no one made a move. The man at the desk was saying something funny and the others were laughing.

After a few minutes more of conversation, one of the young men left the group and came through the door, closing it behind him.

"You want something?" he asked.

"Yes," David replied, annoyed and wanting to say, "Of course I want something."

Instead he said, "I am Dr. David Andrew Williams,

licensed to practice in the state of New York. I believe I am qualified by reciprocity for this state. I would like to check on that and do whatever is necessary to be licensed."

"What you say your name is?"

David told him and said, "I passed the New York State board three years ago."

Without another word the man turned and walked back through the door. When he came out again he said, "You can go in." The balding head of the man at the desk was bent over a folder. The man did not acknowledge the presence of a visitor. The others had left the room. There were no paper cups in sight.

Finally the man at the desk looked up. "You are David Andrew Williams?"

David nodded.

"I see you did qualify in New York, three years now. What have you been doing since then?"

"I was at Bellevue, intern and resident. That duty terminated June thirtieth. Now I want to complete any procedures for license to practice here."

"You mean in this city, instead of New York?"

"In this state," David answered. "In Pocahontas County; I've always wanted to return to South Town for my practice. That's my home."

"Is the hospital there putting you on staff?"

"I hope to have a general practitioner's relationship with the Boyd Memorial Hospital, but I plan to have my own office set up, in the country really, outside of town."

There were a few more questions. Then David was given a set of forms to be completed.

"I guess you've thought this all out," the man said, "I mean setting up in the country and in the South."

David agreed that he had thought it out.

Junior was waiting for him. He was lying on the grass in the shade of one of the great oak trees across the street. The car was parked two blocks away. It was a hot day for a walk. David slipped out of his jacket and opened his collar.

Junior wanted to know how it went.

"Oh, very well," was the answer. "I have to fill out some papers, but everything will be O.K."

"Did they say 'Welcome back to your old home state'? Anything like that?"

"Well, hardly. Perhaps they were a little surprised."

He did not give details of his reception.

He wanted to go next to the Methodist Hospital. The hospital had a close relationship with the state medical college. It was one of the several medical schools to which he had applied while he was an undergraduate. He had not been accepted.

"Funny," he said to Junior, "maybe if they had known I was black they would have let me in."

"Don't you mean if they had *not* known you was black they would have admitted you?"

"No. That's what's funny about it. Lots of things all twisted up like that in today's world."

Junior had to have an explanation.

David gave it: "On the application there was nothing to indicate race. I guess that's the law. For a while they had a place for a photograph, but now they don't even use that way to screen applications."

"Yes," Junior said, "then they could bypass those who showed up black in their pictures."

"There was the case of one black student who filed application and pasted in the picture of a white boy. He was accepted, and when he showed up all hell broke loose. They tried to bar him, alleging fraud and misrepresentation and all that."

"What happened?"

"The guy who was applying had already alerted the N.A.A.C.P. Their lawyers took up the case. The picture was not signed. The applicant had never said 'This is a picture of me.' He just pasted it in a space which was marked 'Photograph.' The school backed down and tried to forget about it. The case never even went to court."

They talked about that, and then as they rode toward Methodist Hospital David said, "But that wasn't the case with me. At the time I was filing applications a lot of med schools were falling all over themselves trying to recruit black premeds. My college adviser suggested that although there was no place on the application papers for a photo I ought to staple my picture on."

"Sure, and make them know you played football"—Junior was laughing—"maybe a picture out of a newspaper with you snagging a pass. I bet that would impress some folks."

"Of course I didn't do it."

"I think I would have," Junior said. "Our people have missed so much that when there's some advantage in being black I think we deserve it."

"Well, I got in on my school record. It wasn't outstanding but I had a choice of three med schools, and then for intern I applied all around and I was accepted at Bellevue. So now you know the story of my life," he concluded as they pulled up in front of Methodist Hospital.

There was a distinct flurry of excitement when he said at the information desk that he was Dr. David Williams from New York. A supervising nurse left other staff persons behind the desk. With a pleasant smile she asked what they might do for him.

He told her that he planned to establish his practice near South Town and that he wished to be acquainted with Methodist Hospital. Within minutes he was in the office of the hospital administrator, who expressed his hearty welcome. The two men were soon joined by a Dr. Tennant, the hospital's chief of staff.

Both men were especially interested in the fact that

Dr. Williams was going to take skills from the big city hospital into the country. They invited him to use their services.

"It is fortunate for us that you should come in just now," Dr. Tennant said. "We are completing our plans for a new service of outreach. It is still experimental to some extent, but we will have a television-by-telephone system between our plant and selected offices. We hope you'll be interested in cooperating."

He explained that the hospital specialists and technicians would be able to view on a screen a patient in the outreach office. They could examine X-ray plates and watch an operation as it took place.

Dr. Tennant spoke of the Boyd Memorial Hospital in South Town. He had visited there to talk about the outreach program, but Dr. Boyd had not been interested. He felt that he and his staff were quite able to deal with all their cases.

"Of course," Williams said, "I believe their chief surgeon, Dr. Von Schilling, is a good man. I won't be having any such setup. I'll be glad to accept all the help I can get."

Dr. Tennant took Dr. Williams for a tour of the wards, operating rooms, nursery, and other facilities of the Methodist Hospital. It was by no means as large as Bellevue, and, David was glad to observe, it was not as crowded and the staff was not as rushed.

As they were moving toward the front door, Dr. Tennant stopped to greet two men who were entering. He introduced David to them. They were ministers of churches in the city. Dr. Tennant told them that David was going to set up in the rural section of Pocahontas County.

"That's a real missionary spirit," one of them said.

David laughed. "No," he answered, "I can't get credit for that. I'm just a country boy going back home, that's all."

The next morning David went again to the Boyd Memorial Hospital. The receptionist greeted him cordially. He heard her announce him by telephone to Boyd's secretary.

"Dr. Williams from New York is here to see Dr. Boyd."

When he was shown into the inner office, Harold did not rise from his seat behind the wide desk. With little more than a nod in greeting, Harold started talking loudly and rapidly as though he were afraid David was going to ask a favor of him.

"David Williams, you know I told you we can't use you on our staff. It just wouldn't work with our people and we don't have enough of your people to support a special unit. Like I told you before, you ought to settle up north somewhere. They got the money up there and you can make it, and if you want to do charity work you can spend some time in the free clinics and in the ghetto. We got nothing for you here. We don't need you in South Town."

As Harold slowed down, David answered with equal force. "You must be forgetting that I told you I wasn't looking for a job in your hospital. I wouldn't want a job anywhere. But I am going to practice in this county. I've asked the state board to issue my license and I'm negotiating for a place about twelve miles from here. All I ask is the usual cooperation in admission of my patients in event of emergency, and the privilege of following them in a courtesy staff relationship."

"That will have to be further considered," Harold answered. "My board of directors has to verify the qualifications of any doctor who comes in here, regular staff or courtesy."

"My qualifications will be established." David was completely confident. "The State Board of Medical Examiners will have documentation from my medical school and from the hospital where I have been."

"You still can't be certain about the state board. There are a lot of factors they take into consideration."

"I'll meet their criteria."

"But I thought when you were here before that you would have sense enough to see that it's not really practical to set yourself up as a country doctor. It would be hard enough for a white man. You can't do it, Williams. You'll see."

"You might remember my father." David Williams got to his feet as he said it. "He used to say to me, 'Don't let nobody tell you what you cannot do.' He said a lot of other things too, and maybe some of them I don't remember, but I can't forget that. I won't take more of your time now, Dr. Boyd, but I will be around."

Seventeen

David Williams spent time with John Manning talking about building and construction. Although Manning's condition made it impossible for him to perform the tasks of a builder, he knew how the work should be done and he knew county supply sources and people who had special skills.

With a drawing board before him he took a pencil in his crooked fingers and sketched as he talked.

"We don't know the dimensions of your building," he said, "but we can get them later. We can think about a floor plan, the layout of your rooms, and the changes to be made in your front elevation."

Starting with the supposition that the building was some sixty feet across the front, they decided on a possible floor plan. In spite of his handicap Manning's lines were straight and clean. They considered an entrance lobby at the center and a reception area with a counter, and behind the counter office space with file cabinets. Then, to the right, a waiting room. From the waiting room a passage would lead at the back of the office toward the doctor's first consultation room; behind that would be an examination room. Next to the examination room would be a smaller room with X-ray equipment. They discussed how these rooms would be utilized.

David took the drawings home with him, working over them, anxious to go back to take measurements but allowing himself only a passing glance as he drove by, guessing frontage and the depth of the structure.

He stayed up nights long after the others. They were accustomed to early-to-bed and early-to-rise country living. His days were long. After the house was quiet he would be working, trying to figure materials, two-by-fours for partition walls, plywood sheeting, insulation between some of the partitions, windows, metal-framed, some of them with louvers. Furnaces, oil-burning for heating and for the hot-water supply, toilets, basins, and slop sinks. He examined his glossy catalogues put out by the supply houses. He saw the prices demanded and at times he shuddered to think of the cost of equipping his place. He did not try to list prices and strike a total, but he knew he would have heavy debts by the time he was set up.

He found himself staying up long after the night plane had gone over. If he heard it, he would recognize the time and perhaps slow up and go to bed. Some nights, in his concentration, he did not hear its soft hum swelling and fading again.

The waiting was not easy.

The uncertainty about the acquisition of the Haywood property gave the young doctor a real experience in tension.

"Oh, eat your dinner, boy," Velvet said at the table on Friday. "You got no cause to worry. You going get the place, God helping you. I see you in there, every time I close my eyes, waking or sleeping." Her eyes closed and her hands started moving through the air. "I see you in your white coat, sitting at your desk and looking at a lady with a little boy on her lap."

Angie said, "Oh, Ma."

Israel looked over and said, "Shut up, girl."

"Then I see you over a operating table," Velvet went on, "and there is nurses all around you, and you reach up and one of them nurses puts a knife in your hand and you looking at just the right place. . . ."

"Go, Ma, go"—Junior was rolling with laughter.

Ruthie said, "Mom's been looking at them doctor T.V. shows. . . ."

Even David had to laugh.

Velvet opened her eyes. "Never mind," she said, "never mind. I know what I'm seeing and I know what going to happen. This ain't the first time, either."

"Ma, that's just superstition," Jocelyn said.

"Can't tell, Jocie," David said. "You can't be too

sure about that." He turned toward Velvet and he said, "You know, I am truly hoping you're right."

The next morning, Saturday, before the family's weekly trip into town, the telephone rang. It was for David.

Dr. Hart was calling.

He had been to the recorder's office and checked title to the property. It was free and clear. He had called on Haywood's agent and worked out a deal. David was to meet the seller to sign the contract at the county courthouse on the following Monday at eleven o'clock. He was to have with him a cashier's check for forty-five hundred dollars made out in favor of Jefferson Davis Haywood. Hart said the spelling of the name was important, and he went over it while David wrote it out.

As David turned from the telephone and told the others what had been said, Israel let out a whoop and Velvet grabbed him and hugged him.

"Man, you got it!" Israel said.

"I told you so," Velvet was saying over and over. "I told you so."

Junior and the girls shared in the celebration. At the back door Woolford started barking at the noise inside. He seemed to know that everybody was happy.

On Monday morning at the courthouse David was parking on the south side of the square at the same time that Hart was parking his car on the north side.

They saw each other. They were both ahead of time and they walked to the center of the square, meeting at the monument raised, according to the bronze plaque, "To the Memory of Our Brave Confederate Dead."

David was trying to hold his emotions under control, but Israel beside him was excited and happy and curious.

"We ready, Dr. Hart," he said, "we sure ready. Hope everything comes out."

Hart gave assurances that once the contract was signed and the contract money was paid they could be assured the deal would be completed.

David handed the check, in a bank envelope, to Hart and said, "I didn't understand the amount. We were prepared to pay a little more, ten per cent of the purchase price.

Hart's head went to one side. He did not smile, but his face showed he was pleased.

"Oh, didn't I tell you?" he asked. "We negotiated the price. The actual contract price is forty-five thousand dollars instead of fifty thousand. That leaves you a bit for your expenses."

They entered the courthouse, and Hart led them to the office of the county clerk in the back of the building.

An old man seemed to be expecting them. He led them into an inner office, a conference room where chairs were in place around a long table.

As they were getting seated, the old man left them. It was eleven o'clock. A younger man came in. He was tall and thin. His head was a shock of red hair. He was smiling as he walked toward David with his hand out.

"David Williams! Am I glad to see you, man!"

"Little Red!" David exclaimed. A flood of memories returned. There had been an adventure at the swimming hole when David went to the rescue of "Red" Boyd, Harold Boyd's cousin, and the two of them were swept over the dam.

Little Red, now using his full name, John Campbell Boyd, was working for his uncle, the banker. He was representing Haywood, and he had conducted the negotiations with Hart.

Haywood was late. David and Red, as they called each other with affection, talked about their lives since they had last met.

In addition to working for Mr. Boyd, Red was reading law under the guidance of a practicing attorney. He hoped to qualify for the state bar. David described a little of his life.

The door opened again and Jefferson Davis Haywood entered the room. In a suit of blue serge, with a white shirt and a thin necktie, he hardly looked like a country storekeeper.

For a moment he stood in the door, and grunts and puffs came from him as Red Boyd jumped up and went to meet him. The others spoke their good mornings. He said nothing until he was seated at the table, with Red at his side. David, Israel, and Dr. Hart sat across from the seller and his agent.

"I'm being robbed," Haywood said. "Yessir, you all got together to rob me." Red said something to quiet the old man. "Never mind, boy, you too. You joining with them niggers to rob me, I'm a white man. You're a white man. You all robbing me out of my good land; ought to go for hundred thousand or more. You all taking it up for peanuts."

Red Boyd talked to soothe his client. He said that they had gone over everything before. The price was less than the price for prime farmland, well located, but Haywood's property was not prime farmland and it was not well located.

"Like I told you," he concluded, "you're mighty lucky in that Dr. Williams can make use out of the land and that he can afford to give you a fair price, so you can go off and enjoy your retirement."

"Being robbed," Haywood said again as Red spread the papers before him and began to point out the details. Hart put his copy of the contract in front of David, and he laid the check face-up on the table.

Back at the house later, Velvet and Junior wanted to hear all the details. Israel told the story with his own flourishes.

"You should of saw the old man's face," he concluded, laughing as he remembered. "I know that Dr. Hart put the check out there so he could see it, kind of so he could even read that long special legal name of his on it and the amount. He quieted down some, kept on saying under his breath 'Niggers robbing me,' but when Red Boyd showed him where to sign he signed right off and grabbed for the check, but Dr. Hart pulled it back. Waited until the old man signed all the papers, then Dr. Hart looked them all over, reading everything slow-like. He had David sign all the papers like he supposed to. Finally he picked up our copies of the papers and then he slid the check over to young Mr. Boyd. Old Man Haywood snatched for it. Said like since he was being robbed he might as well have what little bit there was for him."

The contract provided that the buyer should have reasonable access to the property for inspection and that surveyors should clearly delineate the boundaries. The transaction was to close in thirty days.

Before they left the courthouse David had final instructions. Hart told him to proceed with plans, to make his inspections, take measurements, order materials, and to be ready to take possession in thirty days.

"But you haven't said just how much you might secure on a mortgage," David said. "I don't know what we will have to put up."

Hart was not at all disturbed.

"With what you told me you would have, there will

be enough to meet the requirements," he said. "In the meantime I'll be doing the best I can. First I'm going to apply to North Carolina Mutual in Durham."

"Oh, I know"—David recognized the name. "That's the insurance company. My folks had policies with them as long as I can remember. My father's life insurance was with them."

"Well, that's good to know." Now Hart did smile. "And what was his name?"

David gave the names of both his parents and that of his sister.

"I think I'll just drive on to Durham today," Hart said. "Might as well get this application filed. Fact is, they'll be happy to hear from an old policyholder."

They did proceed to take measurements. John Manning carried a clipboard in the crook of his arm and made notes and sketches and set down figures. Junior came along to hold the tape line and to help however he might. Junior was surprised to see that the estimate of sixty feet across the front was almost exactly right. Other estimates were close too.

"What about the front?" Junior asked. "You going to have all those open windows like Old Man Haywood had?"

"No. We sure don't have anything to display," David answered. "Most of the front will be closed, main entrance at the center, exit doors at both ends, and windows with glass set into metal frames, probably louvered windows."

"What windows?"

"Louvers—you know, glass strips that open like shutters."

Junior had seen them, but he had never known the name of them.

Israel's "stick" carpenter was brought in. He would be glad to help.

"He can't figure so much on paper," Israel said, "but he makes his order, and then when he finishes the job, like he don't have no leftovers."

In the planning they had to figure on electric outlets and high-voltage circuits for special equipment. David had an electric contractor come in and go over the plans. It was like that, too, for the plumbing.

"Plumbing is a 'guzinto' business," David said to Junior. He explained: "Plumbing is a matter of joining up from supply to place of use, and from place of use outward to disposal, and the main thing is 'This goes into that,' and that's why we say it's a 'goes into' business. Now, perhaps I would know all the goes-into's making up the fittings and joints, and threading pipe and pouring lead, but that's not in my field. So we'll get the contractors in."

"I get it," Junior said. "All this is outside plumbing and you're an inside-plumbing man."

"Right on." David had to laugh as he extended the joke, "Or you might say that a doctor is an inside man plumber."

The building which had served the community for many years as a general store had a character of its own. It was both wider and deeper than it had been originally. It was built high to avoid dampness from the heavy rains. The wide porch across the front was some six feet above the ground. The approach from the ground was by wooden steps. Practically the whole front wall could be opened in good weather, with panel sections hinged at the top and hooked into the porch wall. It gave the building the appearance of an open-air market. Those who passed on the road could see the merchandise offered for sale. At one time the stock had been large and varied, but those days were in the past. Haywood had little more to sell or to give away.

Junior considered himself the general helper, runner, messenger, and taker of notes, and possibly a first assistant to Dr. Williams.

"I want to get everything down on paper!" David told Junior. "An architect would make the drawings look prettier, but I believe that with a little help from you and John Manning we can do as well. Of course, we'll have to make changes as we go along."

"Well, with all this space I'm sure you'll have

enough room," Junior said. "I never realized the building was so big."

"But I'll need all the space there is," David replied. His plans were not complex. Partitions would be made with two-by-four framing. Prefabricated door and window casings would be set into the framing.

"Plumbers and electricians will be running their lines as fast as we get the framing set up," David explained. "Then we'll finish off with pre-finished plywood, something in light color, maybe birch. We'll make sure the floor is leveled off, may have to put down new flooring some places and sand down some others. Then we put down asphalt tile. Overhead we'll have a sound-absorbent ceiling, eight feet everywhere, with fluorescent lights in most of the area and special working lamps where they're needed."

John Manning was like a person coming out of retirement.

"Man, I know how it's got to be done," he said, "only these twisted-up hands won't let me execute. I got to help the doctor get going here so he can work on me. How about the heavy equipment? Aren't some of these things, like X-ray and all, pretty heavy? Don't you think we ought to strengthen foundations and underpinning?"

"You're sure right, John," David answered. "We may have to put down some concrete footing and heavy timbers. We don't want anything falling through."

"How about the sewage disposal?" Israel asked. "Have you and the plumbing contractors figured how you'd lay that out?"

"We'll have to have a septic tank, something like a dry well," David answered, "and with a supplemental disposal field. It will all be downhill from the building. Over the dry well will be an ornamental flower garden, and the disposal field will be under a plot of grass."

From the signing of the contract in mid-July to the closing date, things moved swiftly. A lending officer came from the insurance company to inspect the property. He also checked the plans for improvements. Two days later Hart telephoned to say that the company was willing to grant a mortgage loan of thirty-six thousand dollars.

Israel promised to supervise planting and harvesting and selling some of the timber. "That farmland will take care of itself and pay off the mortgage," he said. "I'll manage it for you, or if you'd rather, I'll buy it off of you. Either way it will be good business."

Eighteen

Joyce Palmer telephoned. She was in her office at the community college. "I'm not teaching this summer but I'm back for a few days," she said. "I'm trying to work out a proposal for a research project and I need all the help I can get."

David answered that he, too, was back, but he was back to stay and he also needed all the help he could get. Joyce described her idea for a study of the changing attitudes among black and white people in the South.

"This area is a perfect laboratory," she said. "I want to measure and classify the effects of civil rights legislation, integration and all."

David described his activities and the need to make plans.

"What you're doing sounds exciting," she answered. "Maybe I should be helping you, or anyway seeing what you're doing."

It was agreed that she would drive over the next day.

Velvet was immediately interested. Would she be coming for lunch? The answer was no. Then would she stay for dinner? David could not be sure. He had not asked.

Velvet complained, "Men is so thoughtless, but of course I'll have a little something so she won't go away hungry."

In the morning David was busy with a plumbing contractor. When he got back to the house after twelve o'clock, he saw that Velvet and the girls had thoroughly cleaned the whole place. In his rooms the floors had been waxed. Windows had been washed and fresh curtains were hung. In his bathroom he hardly dared dry his hands on the embroidered guest towels.

"Nothing special," Velvet said. "I don't want no visitor coming here and thinking we keep a dirty house. Besides, I got to get the rooms fixed up a little for your mamma and Betty Jane."

"But that will be two or three weeks yet."

"Well, it ain't worthwhile to wait 'till the last minute."

Israel and Junior worked at the farm during the morning. After they ate lunch Velvet had them bathe and put on clean clothes.

When Joyce drove into the yard only David and the dog Woolford were in sight to meet her. David knew that the lady professor was under close inspection as she got out of the car. He thought she looked like a happy child. Her response to his kiss was warm. She was wearing a simple yellow dress with a matching sun hat. Her bare brown shoulders and arms were in sharp contrast to the bright yellow.

As they moved toward the house Joyce expressed pleasure in everything she saw—Velvet's flower beds, the swing on the wide porch, and David's look of robust health.

In the living room David made the introductions. It seemed that she was accepted immediately as a friend. Questions flowed between them. Velvet poured iced lemonade and the girls passed the glasses. They soon felt well acquainted.

"I'm going to show Miss Palmer our drawings and then we're going over to the place," David said.

"I bet she'll have some good ideas for you," Velvet said.

"Uncle David," Junior said, "could be you'll have to tear up the papers and start all over again."

Joyce said that wouldn't be nice and Israel said he reckoned David would be willing.

In response to an invitation from Velvet, Joyce said yes, she would be glad to stay for dinner if it wouldn't be too much trouble, and if she wouldn't be in the way.

With that remark she looked at David, and everybody laughed.

David led the way to his section of the house. When he spread out the drawings she could hardly imagine how anything was going to be.

"I'd like to see the place," she said, "the buildings and all, then I'll understand the drawings better."

They spent the rest of the afternoon at Haywood's and she did suggest changes. One was that toilets for men and women should be more available to those in the waiting room. "People, especially sick people," she said, "should not have to ask. It makes them feel they are not really welcome, and besides, they should not be delayed."

Another change—and this too was approved by David—was the location of his own office. "It would be better to have it far back in the building," she said. "The patient, as well as the doctor, needs privacy. It will be quiet back there, and the walk from the waiting room will lend to the feeling of privacy."

She asked some questions and David found himself asking for her opinion about several things. He told her that she was a real help.

Later, at dinner, everyone was completely at ease. It was as though Joyce Palmer, the lady professor, had been a friend of the family for a long time, or as though she, as well as David Williams, were members of the Crawford family.

After she left Velvet said, "I truly do like that young woman. She's got education but she's got sense too."

David's mother was selling the house in North Town. The deal was to close the first week in August. Betty Jane, David's sister, would drive down with her as soon as the business was completed.

"I know people is coming to see your folks," Velvet told David. "They be coming from all over the county, and outside too. I'll have to be ready to give them a bite."

People did come. Some were waiting in the house on the day Betty Jane drove into the yard with Mrs. Williams. It was the first time they had been there in more than fifteen years. It was on a Thursday. On Friday and Saturday many more came, and on Sunday morning Oak Grove Baptist Church was filled to overflowing. It looked like a convention. The minister said he was cutting his sermon short because the Lord had sent another messenger and they all wanted to hear from her.

One of the older members, Sister Padmore, shouted out, "Amen! Amen! Amen!"

People laughed.

After his short sermon the pastor asked Sister Mary Ellen Williams to walk down to the front. Many called their greetings and waved and clapped their hands.

Mrs. Williams expressed her thanks for the privilege of returning to Oak Grove Church to be once more among friends she had always loved. She spoke of her life as a child and of unforgotten lessons from the

Sunday school. She remembered her marriage at the altar there and she spoke quite calmly of the death of her husband, whom she described as "a fine Christian man whom many of you knew and loved." She spoke of her parents, whose bodies were in the hallowed ground at the side of the church.

David had always known his mother had a gift for making others share her deepest feelings.

She said she was especially thankful for her son and her daughter. She felt that both of them had the strength and the high-reaching faith of their father. They had dedicated their lives to service.

Sister Padmore and others called their amens. Some were crying. David could not keep back his own tears.

After the benediction almost all the older people reassembled at the Crawford home. The only reason Velvet did not run out of food was that she had prepared to receive visitors for a week or more. Also, some who came brought food with them.

Betty Jane said that when they had moved away she was "only a little kid." She had never realized the love the people had for the family. She did have memories of the church and the school in South Town. She could appreciate the changes. She talked about moving back to the South. She checked and found that salaries for teachers were almost as high as in the North.

She met Joyce and she liked her.

"David," she demanded, "what are you waiting on?

She would make you a wonderful wife, and she likes the South. She likes you too. I can tell that."

David pleaded that he was too busy to think about getting married. "Later," he said, "when I get into my place and I'm able to think about something more than building and plumbing and equipment and prices. Wow! You wouldn't believe what these costs are mounting up to. I can't think about taking on a wife to support too. Not now."

Betty Jane said he was just as crazy as he had always been, but he'd better not put off asking that girl, because she was worth going after. "I'd really like to have her for a sister-in-law," she said.

As the date of the closing approached, Mr. Haywood's attitude mellowed somewhat. He complained about people disturbing him, but no one heard him say any more that he was being robbed.

He sold some of his furniture and he gave some to friends.

On the day of the closing he drove away with his daughter in a new Ford van.

"Probably get me a little place down by the water not too far from Charleston," he said. "If you get down that way, look me up."

Building material was delivered on that day, and the next day the work began.

Nineteen

The work went rapidly. John Manning had recruited carpenters. Israel had a crew of laborers whom he directed. The loaded trucks arriving on the morning of the first day brought lumber, nails, plywood, fiberboard, and ready-to-set-in windows and doors.

Hart had done a good job in arranging for financing. The insurance company had loaned eighty per cent of the purchase money. Mrs. Williams had been able to supply the balance from her savings and the sale of the North Town house. Israel said he was willing and able to lend as much as necessary for the improvements. He and Velvet wanted to advance the money without interest, indeed without careful records, but David would not accept help on those terms. "It's plain business," he said. "I'm glad to have your help, but I'll want to pay it all back in time, and with interest."

He had a heavy weekly payroll to meet and material

had to be paid for as it was delivered. David was surprised to see how prices of almost everything had risen.

But the sounds of construction were in the air, the pounding of hammers, the whine of power saws, the calls between workers. People who had heard about Dr. Williams drove from all over the county to see. Those who came first spread the word. It was a local wonder. Others who chanced to drive by were surprised to see so much action at Haywood's corner.

One farmer stopped his car and leaned out to call, "What's going on here? What you all making?"

One of the laborers answered, "We making a doctor's office."

David, passing by with a sheaf of papers under his arm, stopped and turned toward the car. He was wearing the white overalls of a carpenter. A sweat-dampened T-shirt was tight across his brawny shoulders.

"Is that right?" the farmer asked. "Doctor's office? What for a doctor going to set up here?"

"Well, I guess folks around here need a doctor just like in any other place," David answered.

"He must be some kind of a nut," the man said. "Folks around here got no money, and them that has go on in town to Dr. Boyd's Hospital."

"But them that don't have money, they still need a doctor sometimes."

"Some kind of a nut, probably," the farmer said. He drove off, shaking his head from side to side.

Friends came. They were surprised, surprised to see how fast the changes were being made, and surprised to see how much Dr. Williams knew about making the changes.

However, the work was not going as fast as he had hoped. When he had worked big construction jobs during summer vacations, everything moved faster. Much of the work was mechanized, and the workers were specialists in certain tasks. Floor layers moved like automatons. Framers did nothing but framing. Roofers moved across the tops of houses in waves. Supplies were lifted from the ground by elevators.

"Machines are doing lots of the work," he told Junior, "and the men who operate the machines call themselves engineers."

On this job men worked with hand tools. They talked together and sometimes they sang. They never hurried.

Still, he saw the main building and the residence up the hill at the rear shaping up. His mother was often at the house, which was to be the home for her and the son of whom she was so proud. She admired the bathroom which was being installed and she had her own ideas about the layout of the kitchen—cabinets and plenty of storage space. No partitions had to be installed there, but all the walls and all the woodwork, doors and window frames were freshly painted.

"We won't try to decorate just now," David said to his mother. "We'll just be making everything clean. After we get in, we can worry about color schemes and maybe we'll want wallpaper instead of paint."

Joyce visited often. She was studying for her Doctor of Philosophy degree.

"I don't have to spend a lot of time in classes," she told David. "Lots of reading to do, research, and I want to develop a really significant project."

"I've got one for you," David said with a slow smile. "It's sociological and psychological. What makes things move so much slower in the South than in the North?"

"You mean they don't push themselves as hard as you would like them to." Joyce was quite sure she knew the answers. "You've been away too long. I've just arrived, but I believe I can answer without research."

"Well, it's not only that."

"Yes, these people aren't motivated, and too, they don't have the experience and the general know-how of the North. Besides, it isn't so much the North as it is the city. The differences lie between rural and urban areas even more than between northern and southern."

"But it's not only that." David had a point he wanted to make. "Take the people up there in Capital City, the Board of Medical Examiners. I still haven't got my clearance to practice in the state. They've had plenty of time to check me out. When I went into the office it looked like they were having a party. Staff was jolly and comfortable. I just had to wait."

"Might it not be that your papers from Bellevue and the New York board were delayed?"

"No, it can't be." David had asked when he was in the office. They already had everything from New York.

There were more delays. In September some of the workers had to return to their farms or to the plots which they worked on shares. The principal delay was with the plumbing. Contractors had not received supplies. A hot-water boiler which came was not the one they had ordered. It was too small to supply the office building and the home on the hill.

Medical equipment came and the suppliers sent in technicians to set it up. A graduate nurse, Grace Pegram, whose family David had known as a boy, applied for work. She was employed at the Methodist Hospital but said she believed she would be happier in the country. David said she could give notice on her job and start working as his nurse on the first of October. He was assured by the contractors that everything would be in order by that time.

The water was not turned on but Mrs. Williams did not want to wait. She and David moved into the house which Haywood had occupied with his family. The new bathroom sparkled with chrome and tile. The modernized kitchen with a stainless steel sink had fluorescent lighting fixtures screened by ground-glass ceiling panels.

Mrs. Williams was completely happy. "I'm not worried that we don't have water," she said. "I lived half of my life without running water in the kitchen and without a bathroom. I can bring water from a well and I can take care of everything in the small house out back without worrying. I wasn't that spoiled living in North Town."

David called the Board of Medical Examiners and learned that everything had not cleared, but no one told him what was left to be done.

In the last week in September he drove again to Capital City. He went to the office of the medical examiners without making an appointment. From the receptionist he got the impression that his visit was expected. She told him that he would have to see Mr. Yarbrough, the executive secretary of the board, but he was in conference.

"I'll wait for him," David said. He was determined not to be put off.

He seated himself in one of the luxurious overstuffed

lounge chairs. The young woman rose and walked out of the room.

She was soon back, saying, "You can go on in now."

"Well, Doctor," Yarbrough said brusquely, "we have told you that you will be notified when the board passes on your application. These things take time, you know. And there are still some unanswered questions in your case."

"There are?"

"No further questions for you to answer"—Yarbrough showed confusion. "So far as I know you have done everything required."

"What, then? I'd like to know what questions there are. I've had my own problems down there in South Town with county building inspectors and with contractors and with some of the workers. Still, my place is ready. I want to open the office on the first day of October. And there are people, lots of them in the area, who need medical services. So what are the unanswered questions?"

"Well, I don't suppose you're the one who could answer them."

"I'm the one being held up. It is my problem and I want to know."

"We have to get verifications, investigate the things you have told us. You know how that is."

"I can't say that I do. I'm sure that my school

records have been verified, and that records of my internship and residency must have been verified."

"Well, it's not that."

"What, then? I've got to know. And how much more time will it take?"

"I don't think I should be telling you anything more." Yarbrough looked out the window, then he turned back. "Have you been having some trouble locally? Like in the profession?"

"No, of course not."

Yarbrough rose from his seat and went to a file drawer. He came back, and as he sat he turned sheets, forms, carbon copies, and replies. Finally he spoke. "You said that you would be using the facilities of the Methodist Hospital here in Capital City, and also the Boyd Memorial in South Town. Did you ever clear any arrangements, especially at Boyd Memorial?"

"Clear?" David remembered only too well his visits to the two hospitals.

"You understand your application has not been denied," Yarbrough said. "It will be considered by the Board of Examiners at the next meeting. That will be on October Eighth."

"Yes," David answered. "I believe I do understand."

On the way back from the city he drove in deep thought. At the Alberta turnoff he took the road to the right and started for the community college. He gave his name in the office and asked if Miss Joyce Palmer might be able to see him. The office staff seemed to know who he was. They asked him to be seated while one of the clerks left the office. She was back in a few minutes with Joyce, who led him to her own office. She closed the door and turned to him.

"What is it, David?" she asked, "what's wrong?"

"Oh, please excuse me"—he tried to smile—"I didn't mean to let it show."

"What is the trouble? Sit down. Tell me. I have nearly an hour before my next class."

He told her in a few words. She listened without interrupting until he stopped. Then she spoke.

"You say you've been to the hospital and you've talked to Dr. Boyd? Then he knows your plans and your need to have a working relationship with the hospital?"

David nodded.

"Who else at the hospital is important? Anybody on staff who might influence him one way or the other?"

"No. No one on staff, but there's his father, who practically owns the hospital, and Harold Boyd spoke of the hospital board—that would be nobody but Old Man Boyd."

"So, why don't you go to the father? Show him what you're doing and ask for his cooperation."

"That's just what they would like to see me do." David felt his anger rising with the memories that flooded back. "Harold's father once said that he could drive my father from the county, and that my dad would come back crawling and begging for a chance to work. Well, my daddy did leave the county but he never begged for anything from Old Man Boyd, and I'm not about to crawl for him or for his son."

"I see." Joyce rose and went to the window. Neither spoke. She returned to her desk and as she seated herself she said, "David, you know you're a proud black man."

He started to protest, but Joyce raised her hand to stop him. "That's not a criticism," she said, "it's a statement of fact, perhaps a judgment, or you might say a diagnosis."

She went on to say that she could understand, and she hoped he would understand.

"I believe I understand very well. I am my father's son and I am not about to beg Harold Boyd or Old Man Boyd or any other white man for anything."

David poured out more of the story of his family's relationship with the Boyd family. He told about his first visit to the hospital, his resentment, unspoken at the time, at Harold Boyd's introduction of him as "this boy whose daddy used to work for my daddy."

Joyce kept him talking, putting in leading questions each time he paused. The hour was almost up when David realized that his anger had subsided.

"Joyce, you are a very wise woman," he said. "Need

I say a very wise black woman? You have had me in treatment for this hour. I should pay you for the therapy."

"Shall I send you my bill?"

"Yes, please do. But don't tell me to go back to see Harold Boyd."

"Don't be stubborn, or too proud, Dr. Williams."

"I'm not stubborn, and I'm not proud, but as a medical doctor I know I am qualified by training and experience, and I don't believe that people like the Boyds can keep me from practicing. I'll get my license with or without their approval. You know this is the New South."

Twenty

The credentials for Dr. David Andrew Williams had not arrived on the first day of October.

That morning Nurse Pegram was in the office ready for work. She looked over the new equipment and said that all of it was of the very best quality and the latest design. She was going to enjoy working with it.

Also present was young Phyllis Manning, a nurse with limited experience. She had worked in the office at Boyd Memorial Hospital. Her uncle, John Manning, had recommended her and he had persuaded her to leave Dr. Boyd's employ. David was helping her to understand the filing system. There were some instruction manuals to be studied.

The telephone rang.

Miss Manning answered, as she had been instructed, "Dr. Williams' office"; then she said, "One moment, please." Turning to Dr. Williams beside her, she said, "It's Dr. Tennant of Methodist Hospital in the city."

Dr. Tennant came on with hearty expressions of congratulations, concluding with, "And you've got a girl who can answer the telephone. Sometimes we don't have that around here."

David answered with thanks but he had to say, "We can hardly say this is a doctor's office. The state board has not yet issued me a license. I phoned the office yesterday. The clerk has said the board would be meeting next week. I'll just have to wait."

There was a pause at the other end of the line, then, "What's that? I thought you took care of that some time ago, more than a month ago, wasn't it?"

"Yes, Doctor," Williams answered. "I did everything I could, filed the papers, made sure that New York sent in copies of my records, but it seems that was not enough."

"Look, Dr. Williams, I really don't understand. I was telephoning to wish you well and also to see if you might invite me over to look at your setup—not an inspection, you know, but just to see how things were shaping up."

David expressed his appreciation, saying that Dr. Tennant was still invited. "Certainly," he said, "I have plenty of time to show my office and the new equipment. I could take you for a tour of the community too. For the present, I have little else to do."

Dr. Tennant said, "You know, I filled out a statement about cooperating with you some weeks ago. I'm sure that went in to the board but I'll check with my secretary." Before he hung up, Dr. Tennant offered to do anything at all to help. He wanted to see the place, but perhaps, he said, that wasn't the most important thing.

David was encouraged by the call. He believed that pressures could be brought on the board of examiners and also on Dr. Boyd. He would not ask anyone to intervene for him. However, if Dr. Tennant or anyone else, on his own initiative, volunteered to help, David believed action would be taken.

People came. John Manning was there early and Israel came later. John talked to the carpenter who was putting a railing around the front porch. Old Man Haywood had never had a railing, and so far as anyone knew, there had never been an accident. But David wanted the porch railing as a protection for children and old people and anyone who might be weak or crippled.

No one understood why Dr. David Williams was not ready to start treating patients, and no one in the office tried to explain.

Velvet and Mrs. Williams outdid each other in trying to clean and polish everything. They oiled the furniture and waxed the floors, and although David insisted that the plywood paneling was pre-finished, they insisted on applying paste wax and rubbing it with soft cloths.

In the afternoon many visitors arrived. Mrs. Williams went to her room and changed from soiled work clothes into a fresh house dress. She knew most of the callers, women from nearby communities. Nurse Pegram led them through the rooms and she explained the specialized equipment: X-ray machines, electrocardiograph machines, and others.

Junior, with some of his friends, arrived after his day at the high school. He already knew most of the equipment and he was proud to show it. In the late afternoon Joyce arrived, and at about the same time some of the local teachers arrived, John Smith from the high school with his wife and others.

Everyone was told only that Dr. Williams was not quite ready to open practice. No explanation was given. There were questions but the answers were indefinite. Some expressed surprise at the delay. "Looks like everything is ready to go," they said.

Joyce did show concern. In reply to her question about his schedule David said, "My plans are working. And there are other plans. They will all work out." He tried to sound confident, but Joyce knew he was deeply troubled.

Only Mrs. Williams was calm and undisturbed. She did not know why the board of examiners had not granted her son a license, but she felt sure that all the affairs of men were in the hands of God and that He would, in His own time, bring to pass that which was good. She believed there was reason for the delay and she said, as often as anyone would listen to her, "All things work together for good to them that love God."

She insisted that God did not plan troubles, but out of troubles good flowed to God's children.

Twenty-One

Disaster came to Pocahontas County on the third night of October. There was the anguish of pain and mangled bodies and death.

The press and radio and television covered the story of the plane crash.

It was the plane that went over South Town every night just after twelve o'clock. People said you could set your timepiece by it. In good weather and in foul, at exactly 12:05 the low hum could be heard, swelling and then fading away as the plane moved southward.

On the night of the crash the pilot had radioed his position as he passed over Washington. There was no record of trouble; some people thought there must have been a bomb on board.

One witness said he happened to be out-of-doors at that late hour. He heard the sound of the jets. It was raining. The sound was more than a hum; it was a roar. Then the plane came on like a shooting star, but the witness said he could see it clearly as it passed low. Fire was streaming from the front section and the roar ended with the sound of a crash which hung in the air and echoed.

People near the crash site said later that the ground itself was shaken. Certainly everyone for miles around heard and felt the vibration which ended in an explosion.

David was in bed. He had just gotten to sleep.

The roar of the jets was deafening as it passed over the house. Even before the final crash and explosion he was out of bed. Switching on lights, he ran down to the front door and looked out into the night. It was raining. It was dark. Then beyond the skyline he saw a flickering glow.

His mother stood beside him at the door. "It must be the night plane," she said. "I was awake. It came down like a scream before it hit. God, all those people!"

"I got to go," David said, running back up to his room to slip trousers over his pajamas and shove his feet into shoes. He tried to remember what he had heard or read or learned firsthand about emergency disaster relief. He had been at Bellevue the night of the Long Island Railroad crash. That was city. He had been in a hospital with all facilities: staff, equipment, experts. This was country. This was like roadside emergency.

When he reached the front door Mrs. Williams was

ready to go with him. She had thrown a raincoat over her head. He grabbed his raincoat as he passed the hall rack. He knew that his mother was able to rise to crisis action. As they hurried down the path from the house to the office building, he told her what to do.

"We've got to get the folks together, Mama. Get on the phone and call Israel. Ask him and Junior to get out to wherever the plane is down. Never mind about coming here. He'll be able to find it. Tell him bring the flat-bed truck. Then call Grace Pegram. Tell her to come too. And Phyllis Manning. Could be some of the people are not dead. Even if they are, we'll need all the help we can get."

As he talked David was gathering the things he would need in the emergency. He unlocked the cabinet where he had put the hypodermic needles and pain-killing morphine and other drugs. He put some of them into his bag.

From another cabinet he took traction splints and boxes of bandages. These, with his bag, he took to the station wagon, and he came back for the two stretchers. He wished he had an ambulance, fully equipped and ready for emergency.

Mrs. Williams started carrying out her orders even before he got his things together. She was on the telephone. Israel and Junior were up. Grace Pegram was up and getting dressed. She would be on the way.

Mrs. Williams left the phone to go back to the house and return with a freshly starched white coat.

"Here, Doctor," she said as she held it up. "Better put this on. You'll need it."

David smiled, but he shrugged out of his pajama jacket and thrust his arms into the white coat, as he said, "You know the state didn't say yet that I can touch an injured person."

"I know you're a doctor, and God knows. The piece of paper don't matter. Not at all."

The blaze on the skyline was like a beacon. Other cars and trucks were on the road. People were out to do what they could. Calls went from driver to driver. There were questions about how to get to the scene of the crash. The distance was greater than it would have seemed. David drove over old Route One to go south and crossed the Stony Creek bridge. At the next intersection he turned west again. The area was rich bottom land, most of it planted to cotton, but on the higher ground stood clumps of trees with perhaps a ten-year growth. Such a stand of timber could help to cushion the impact of a downcoming plane; certainly if it were in a glide the trees might slow its motion.

The radio was on, and it was tuned to the best of the news stations in the area. All the news was about the Middle East, the Far East, the market, and sports, mostly a repeat of early broadcasts.

He kept thinking that the flames were just over the hill. Then, at the top of a long rise, he could see fire just beyond the next ridge. It silhouetted a stand of trees, tall pines like Christmas trees. Other drivers, too, had seen it. A speeding pickup truck overtook the station wagon, passed by, and then braked to a fast stop. Two men jumped out. One, swinging an ax or a sledge hammer, attacked a post in the fencing on the side of the road. He was cutting through the fence so the truck could drive through. He had a post down and he hacked away at the wires. Then he called and beckoned to the driver of the truck. David got out of the station wagon. From under the seat he took flares, and when he got them burning he put them out at right angles to the road. Others coming behind would see the opening. Back at the wheel, he followed as the truck lumbered down into a shallow ditch and climbed up, animal-like, on the other side. In low gear the station wagon bumped over the rough ground.

Reaching the top of the ridge, David saw the bright flames illuminating the last of the fuselage of the tri-motored plane. It stood upended as though it had tried to dive into the earth. A trail of fires extended for a quarter of a mile. David reasoned that the plane, gliding, must have swept over the lower treetops, striking, shearing the tops of taller trees and losing parts of itself as the fuselage was torn open and its load was spilled on a long trail. Another truck and some cars were already there. Those who had arrived were watching the burning remains.

David turned the station wagon toward the right and drove as close as he could to the clearly marked path that the plane had taken on its downward course. He angled his lights in that direction. Then he jumped out and started walking, turning his flashlight in wide arcs.

Rain was falling. The ground and the woods were damp. Perhaps this was an advantage, in that there would be less fire.

Irregular sections of the plane, silvery in the reflection of light, were on the ground, and some were suspended like decorations in the trees.

People who had arrived earlier were calling back and forth, shouting above the sounds of the burning craft and the fire crackling in trees and brush. David moved in the line of the damaged trees and scattered debris from the plane. Two men were bending over a form on the ground.

"Maybe I can help," he said as he stepped up to them. "I'm a medical doctor."

"Sure, Doc," one of them said.

The other spoke. "Looks like he's dead."

There was a bad twist to the form. David checked. There was no pulse. It was the body of a woman, lying face-down.

"Nothing to do here," David said, "but there must be others."

"Why don't they send some ambulances?" one of the men asked.

"And more doctors?" added the other.

"They'll be coming, I'm sure," David said. "I live near here. Let's check and see if there are any we can help."

Together they started searching again.

They came to a group who had found a man on the ground. The others stepped back while David knelt to make hasty examination. The man was unconscious.

"Doesn't seem too bad," he said. "No heavy bleeding. But we ought to get him in out of the rain, try to keep him warm."

"That's my house, right over there," one of the men said. "We could sure get him there and keep him warm."

"We'll have to be very careful moving him," David said. "I've got a couple of stretchers in my station wagon. Come, we can bring them down and get him aboard."

Before he left, he took off his raincoat and spread it over the injured man. He and two of the farmers went for the stretchers.

As they started back, the farmer who had offered his house said, "But Doctor, what you going to do for

more stretchers? Must be more folks down there going
to need help."

"That's true. Well, before stretchers were invented,
folks used doors to move their sick and injured."

"Right. I'd forgot. If you can manage I'll get on over
to the house and me and my folks will be ready when
you get there, and I'll be getting some doors too."

Other volunteers stepped in. There were women
among them and young people, boys and girls. Israel
and Junior came, offering their truck if it could serve
as an ambulance. David said they might use it later.
He knew ambulances would arrive. He only hoped to
provide emergency help and shelter for those who were
still living.

That was first. By the time he got back they had
found another injured man, conscious and in great
pain. David, moving very slowly and with others doing
what they could, got both men on stretchers. He
fastened the straps, and to quiet the man who was
conscious, he gave an injection to relieve the pain.
With some of the others, he carried the injured pair
toward the farmhouse. It was rough going over the
uneven ground. He kept cautioning those who carried
to avoid, insofar as possible, more injury. As they were
going in the door someone from outside called his
name. It was Nurse Pegram.

With the nurse and with those who had helped to

carry, David got both the injured men from the stretchers to beds. From his bag he gave the nurse some medicines which she might use in emergency.

"I'm taking the stretchers and going back," he said. "We may have to put up more people here for shelter until they can be moved by ambulance to one of the hospitals."

By the time David got back to the scene many more people had come. Nurse Manning was one of them.

"Let me carry this, Doctor," she said as she took his bag. All through the hours that followed she was with him, at his side or one step behind him. She had the bag open as he worked. She loaded fresh hypodermic needles when he called for them. She was careful to use the medication which he named and in the exact amounts he ordered.

Highway police cars had their red beacons flashing and their spotlights probing the area. An older officer seemed to be directing others.

"I'm a doctor," David said to the officer. "I've helped to get two injured men into shelter at that house over there. I've told people who want to help to try to keep those who are alive warm and if possible dry. And I've warned them against moving them carelessly."

"That's all right." The officer looked hard at David. "You say you're a doctor?"

"Williams is the name, David Williams, from New York. Just helping in the emergency."

A young man, one of those who had helped carry a stretcher, ran up. "Doctor," he called, "we need you!"

David followed almost at a run. A crowd opened its circle as he approached. A section of three seats from the plane lay upside-down. They told him a man was suspended under the mass, held by a seat belt. They thought he was not conscious, but he seemed to be alive.

David went on his hands and knees crawling under the overturned bank of three seats. The man's white hair was in strong contrast to the redness of his face. Saliva was coming from his mouth but there was no blood.

David backed out. He directed as many men as could get a hold to lift the irregular mass and turn it to normal position. It was not easy. The seats were firmly attached to sections of metal from the floor. The ends of these were imbedded in the ground.

With the seat section in upright position, David moved toward the victim. He was indeed an elderly man. He was gasping for breath. David unfastened the seat belt. The man gulped in fresh air. The red drained from his face.

"The seat belt saved his life," someone said.

It was true. Held in the seat, he had been in a

position of severe strain, but he did not seem to be seriously injured. A little rain in his face was not harmful. Within minutes he was conscious, although dazed. They got him on a stretcher and David fastened the straps.

"Now, if some of you can take him to the farm-house," he said, "the nurse will take care of him. Be easy with him on the way. He may want to get up to help himself. Don't let him. We don't know the extent of his injuries."

There were other victims. Most of them were dead. Heads had been crushed. Necks and backs had been broken. One woman, calling out with fright as well as with pain, seemed to have a broken leg and a broken arm and possibly broken ribs. David got her on a stretcher, and had her taken to the house. He gave her an injection and sent a note with her to Nurse Pegram.

Before the stretchers came back he had sent two more injured people to the house on doors. He had volunteers gather blankets which had been spilled from the plane. Nurse Manning used them to pad the doors and to cover the victims. For straps to hold the patients in place she tore a blanket into strips. Although the doors were awkward, they proved to be useful. Plenty of helpers were on hand. David let six or eight people go with each victim, cautioning them to move gently and if the victim were conscious to keep offering assurances and comfort. David knew that all the injured were in shock to a greater or lesser degree. Nature was taking its own course to minimize suffering. He was glad there was no hysteria. Those about him—the sightseers, the volunteers, the police officers —complained about the lack of ambulances. He himself, without voicing complaint, wondered why it was taking so long for help to arrive.

Even for those who showed no more than bruises, David advised quiet. One young man who might have been a college football player had a bad head wound; nothing else showed. It was a nasty cut, straight across the forehead, and was bleeding heavily. It would have to be sewed, but David did not try to put in sutures. He only put sterile pads over it and bound it tightly. The victim scorned the idea of being carried on a stretcher or door. David asked two of the volunteers to stay close to him. It was not long before the victim sank to the ground. After that he was loaded on a door and taken to the house.

David had been working only on one side of the path the plane had marked out on its last glide. It appeared that the left side of the fuselage was the one which had been ripped open. Most of the spillage was there. But there was more. Some volunteers had crossed over, and from that side came a call for help. With Nurse Manning beside him, David hurried over.

A woman in dungarees said, "Somebody's under there, I'm sure I heard somebody." She was pointing to a wide aluminum piece on the ground.

David bent low and probed with his flashlight. He heard, rather than saw, that someone was there. He crawled in and his light picked up a section of clothing. On his stomach he moved closer and started talking.

"I'm coming," he said, and then he repeated just the two words, "I'm coming, I'm coming." He spoke the words clearly and reassuringly.

He saw that the injured person was a woman. Groaning sounds came from her. A strut attached to the wing section lay across the upper part of her body.

"I'm coming," he said again. "Just wait a few minutes. I'm going for help. You're going to be all right. I'll be back."

The woman's groaning stopped. Her lips moved but no words came from them. David knew that she had heard him.

"Never mind," he said. "Don't try to talk. Listen to me. You are being held down by a piece of metal. I'll get help and you will be out of here. I am a doctor. I'm going now. Don't try to move. Just wait."

The young woman who had first called him had been joined by others. He told them what he had found. He explained that the metal section should be lifted, but slowly and evenly. It would be important to keep the victim from moving as the pressure was lifted. He would go back under the metal. They were to lift as he called to them.

He went back, saying again, "I'm coming now, and there are friends to help."

The woman's eyes were open. Blood was coming from the corner of her mouth. David got into position, with his hand on the particular strut which was across the woman's chest. Then he called to the others to lift slowly. Nurse Manning at the edge of the metal piece relayed the order and he felt the mass going up. The woman did not move. Her eyes closed.

Nurse Manning was at his side, and others stood by ready to help.

He called for a stretcher or a door as he started to examine the victim. There was blood. He ripped through the blouse. Nurse Manning passed scissors to him. He cut open the bra, exposing a wound above the right breast. It was not arterial bleeding. It was something perhaps more dangerous.

"A sucking wound!" he said. "It's bad."

From his bag he took a roll of four-inch adhesive tape. Nurse Manning waited with scissors, and when he peeled off a ten-inch length she cut it and he applied it over the wound, drawing it tight. The nurse cut another strip of the same size. This he applied at right angles over the first strip.

"We'll have to get her to an operating room. Now."

One of the stretchers was being brought in.

"How is she, Doctor?" asked the young woman who had first alerted him. "You going to operate? Is it that bad?"

"It's a sucking chest wound," he said, as he put the stretcher beside the victim and with the help of Nurse Manning got her on it. "A broken rib has punctured the outer wall of the body. Air gets in there and the lung collapses. It can be fatal. We'll have to try to get her into a hospital for surgery."

With volunteers helping, he started walking toward the place where his station wagon was parked. Junior came from somewhere. He ran ahead and got behind the wheel and started the motor.

"Manning," the doctor said to his nurse, "you'll stay in the back with the patient. Don't let her move. We can't wait for an ambulance. We're going to town."

As David got in the car, Junior moved over to let him take the wheel. As he worked the vehicle, now ambulance, across the rough ground he heard the whine of sirens. Before he reached the broken place in the fence he saw the two ambulances from Boyd's Memorial coming in. He thought of stopping them but there would be too many questions to be answered, and he knew he could lose his patient if there were delay. He passed them. His own horn was blasting.

On the road he leaned out and called to a highway

patrol car, "Emergency! I'm a doctor taking a badly injured victim to Boyd Memorial. Give me escort."

He spoke with authority. The state patrolman asked no questions. He opened his siren and moved as swiftly as the oncoming curiosity seekers would permit. He cleared the way for Dr. David Andrew Williams as he took his patient to the Boyd Memorial Hospital in South Town.

Twenty-Two

They could not make speed. In spite of radio broadcasts advising people not to visit the scene of the accident, the roads were crowded.

"Nothing for all these folks to do," Junior said.

"Anyway, those who got there first were a great help," David answered. "People did what they could, everybody."

"They couldn't have done without you, though, Uncle David. You truly got them together. They just wouldn't have known how to move if you hadn't been there."

"I only gave first aid," David said.

"We get first aid in school," Junior said. "Pressure points, artificial respiration, moving injured people, and like that, but what you were doing was lots more, getting folks organized and having them work together. Mrs. Saunders told me she was mighty proud of you."

"And who is Mrs. Saunders?" David asked. "And what reason did she have to be proud of me?"

"You didn't know? That was Mrs. Saunders' house where the injured people were taken. You didn't recognize Mr. Saunders?"

"Should I? No, I didn't. Who is Mr. Saunders?"

"He's a deacon in our church. You must have known the Saunders family."

"Then he's a black man," David said.

"Didn't you see him? Or the folks at the house?" Junior asked.

"I guess I saw him, and maybe the others, but I didn't notice."

As they approached the town, traffic opened for them. It was not easy to keep up with the patrol car. David's foot pressed hard on the throttle and he kept alert for possible emergencies.

He thought about the woman on the stretcher behind him. He wondered if her race might make a difference. Now that he thought about it he realized that she could be a black woman, using the term as people were using it. He had not noticed whether she was white or just light in color.

He put the question out of his mind.

The patrol car was far ahead of him when it made the left turn into South Town's Main Street. David did not try to catch up. He took the turn at low speed and followed up the hill through the business district and a few blocks of quiet residences, and turned into the wide sweep at the hospital. The patrol car was at the emergency entrance.

Dr. Von Schilling was there.

No words were wasted in greetings.

Dr. Williams told Dr. Von Schilling that this victim of the air crash had what appeared to be a sucking chest wound. As attendants drew the stretcher from the station wagon, Dr. Williams went to his patient. She was trying to smile.

"Oh, you're doing fine," he said. "We're going to get you into the hospital and look at your chest. I'm Dr. Williams and this is Dr. Von Schilling." He kept walking beside the stretcher as it was being borne to the examination room. "Dr. Von Schilling will be able to do whatever is necessary. This is the Boyd Memorial Hospital in South Town. Dr. Von Schilling is chief surgeon! He will get some X-rays and then he'll know more about your condition."

He kept talking until the nurse and the attendants had the victim on the table.

"Now, if you'll excuse me," he said, "you can see I've got to get washed up. They'll be taking pictures and getting some information from you, but I'll be back with Dr. Von Schilling in just a few minutes."

Nurse Manning led Dr. Williams to the surgeon's washroom. She laid out towels and surgeon's gowns and caps. He scrubbed his hands and arms. He needed to take a shower but there was not enough time. A few minutes later Dr. Von Schilling joined him. David described the patient's wound and his treatment and gave his reasons for fearing the condition was very serious.

"She must have been under that wing section for some time," he said. "We can't tell how complete the collapse of the lung is. I've been thinking a chest tube should be inserted right away. It's your decision, Dr. Von."

"I'd rather not." Von Schilling was shaking his head from side to side. "She's your patient. I'll be glad to assist."

"It can't be like that, Doctor." It was Williams' turn to shake his head. "I'm not licensed in this state, and I'm certainly not on staff here in any capacity. You're the surgeon. I'll assist if you tell me you need me. I'm not even sure that will be legal, but it is an emergency."

"Doctor, listen"—Von Schilling was holding Williams' arm—"I'm afraid I can't do this. You must understand. I haven't tubed a sucking chest wound in twenty years, not since I came to America. And when I worked it was with glass tubes, not plastic. Suction was supplied by the mouth of the surgeon. It's all different now. And I haven't done it. You must understand that."

It was a hard decision.

Dr. Williams had seen it done as an intern at Bellevue and he had assisted as a resident. It was done often on Saturday nights with stab or gunshot wounds, especially if a rib had been fractured.

Von Schilling kept talking as Williams dried his hands. As he looked up he saw on the wall a framed copy of the oath he had taken. It was a very old pledge ascribed to Hippocrates, a Greek, the father of medicine. It ended:

While I continue to keep this oath unviolated, may it be granted to me to enjoy life and the practice of the art, respected by all men, in all times, but should I trespass and violate this oath, may the reverse be my lot.

A few minutes later the two doctors checked the patient's name and vital statistics from the chart the nurses had prepared. They studied the X-ray films. Three ribs were broken and the lung on the right side had collapsed. With Von Schilling's help, Williams selected from the emergency tray a coil of plastic tubing of appropriate size. He checked the Gumco machine which would provide low-level suction and he gave simple instructions to the two nurses present.

"Mrs. McMillan," Dr. Von Schilling said to the patient, "we must tell you what the situation is." He proceeded to describe the effect of rib fracture when a broken end of a rib penetrates the body wall. Then he told her how Dr. Williams had sealed the opening as soon as he recognized it.

"That which might be called a field treatment is only temporary," he said. "Now we must insert a tube into the chest and draw from the body the air which has been taken in through the wound. It is something less than a major operation but it is a surgical procedure. It may be that you would recover without this treatment, but we advise you to let us do it. There will be some pain. We would use only local anesthetic. We will want to X-ray again after the surgery. We believe it is necessary to proceed at once.

"Do you fully understand all that I am saying?"

Mrs. McMillan smiled and said faintly that she did understand. She said, "Please do whatever you think best, Doctor."

While Von Schilling was talking, Nurse Manning shook talcum powder on Williams' hands and helped him into sterile rubber gloves.

Von Schilling stepped to the table facing the patient and near the wound. He motioned to Williams to take the position at the patient's back where the chest tube was to be inserted.

While Von Schilling stripped off the adhesive tape and closed the primary wound with sutures, Williams sterilized an area six inches from the wound. He made an injection to anesthetize; then with one deft stroke he made an incision, into which he inserted one end of the tube. With swift, sure movements he secured the tube to the body wall, using sutures and sealing with tape. Then he handed the free end of the tube to nurse Manning, who attached it to the suction machine.

As the machine started working, bubbles appeared in the water trap. Williams manipulated the tube. Von Schilling applied his stethoscope to the patient's right side. He smiled and nodded as he heard the returning breath sounds. Williams watched as the ashy pallor of Mrs. McMillan's face gave way to a more healthy color. He also saw that her breathing became less labored. The procedure was working.

No more bubbles were coming through the Gumco machine. They started getting Mrs. McMillan ready to be moved back to X-ray. The whine of an ambulance siren reached them. Those in the operating room were alerted to the arrival of more injured people. Von Schilling, nurses, nursing assistants, and other doctors would be busy. Dr. Harold Boyd would be returning from the scene of the accident.

Von Schilling told the patient that the procedure had been successful. He explained the postoperative care. "It is fortunate," he said, "that Dr. Williams was available."

They were moving the patient from the table to a gurney, a table with rubber-tired wheels, when the door opened. Harold Boyd burst into the room.

"Dr. Von Schilling, what in God's name is happening here?" he demanded, and without waiting for an answer he went on, "How dare you let this black boy put his hands on a patient in my hospital? And a woman! A white woman! How dare you?"

Von Schilling tried to answer. He spoke of emergency, seriousness of the injuries.

Harold Boyd would not listen. He kept up his tirade. "Our whole institution could be ruined by this. As for you, you're through. I won't tolerate your insubordination. You might as well pack your bag now."

He suggested that criminal action might be taken against Von Schilling. All of his words were directed to his own staff member. Harold said nothing to David. It was as though the black doctor were not in the room.

Harold went to the patient. "Madam," he said, "I offer my apologies. What has happened here was only because of the terrible accident. I was out there, doing my duty to save lives. This black boy, he's not a licensed doctor. He had no reason to bother you. . . ."

"You lie!" David said as he stepped around the gurney and moved toward Harold. "You lie, Harold Boyd. I am a licensed doctor, and I'm not a boy. I'm a man, a doctor, and you know it!"

Harold shouted in return, "Not licensed in this state! No right to come in my hospital!"

"In this state and in any other state I have the right

and the duty to preserve life—and that goes for your hospital too."

"Not in my hospital—you'll never work in here again, and maybe in no other hospital in this state."

"Yes, you would try to fix that." He took another step toward Harold. "Yes, I know."

Harold stepped back and raised a hand as if to ward off a blow. "Von, look at him!" he shouted.

"I know what you've tried to do with the state board"—David raised a clenched fist—"I know, and let me tell you: If you keep me out of practice I'll break every bone in your stupid body. I swear I will!"

The fingers of his right hand were opening and shutting. His whole body was tense. It was like the moment in a football game before the snap of the ball to be followed by hard body contact.

Harold backed away. He kept talking. "I'll show you. I'll show you. I'll get you for this. . . . Threatening to kill me. . . ."

David turned away. He said to Von Schilling, "I'm going to get dressed."

"I'm coming with you," Von Schilling said.

"What?" Harold was shouting again. "You mean to walk out of here in this crisis? A dozen ambulance cases coming in! You walk out now and I'll have you up before the highest boards in the land."

David raised his hand in farewell. He bowed to Mrs.

McMillan and walked past Harold to the washroom. Nurse Manning was just behind him. She was crying as she helped him strip off the rubber gloves and get out of his gown.

When they left the building, Junior was waiting in the station wagon. He had heard the loud voices and he sensed the conflict. David took the wheel. He did not answer Junior's questions, and Nurse Manning said nothing as they drove down through the town and out Route One to the crossroad leading to the place where Dr. Williams hoped to be able to serve the people. After he stopped the car he sat for a while and looked at the building.

It was not a hospital. He did not want a hospital. He just wanted to be back there in the country where he might help people with their problems, problems of health and more, all the problems of living and raising children where hate kept people in fear and ignorance and poverty.

He was not prepared for Harold Boyd's next action.

His mother wanted to know everything. Velvet was at the house. Joyce had telephoned. She was going to be there as soon as possible. Israel was still at the scene of the crash. They had the radio and the television on with reports of the major air disaster. It was said that local people had worked heroically to rescue those who had survived.

Junior talked of how his Uncle David had gotten the volunteers together. Besides members of the Saunders family he named others whom they knew.

David was tired and hungry. It was past lunchtime. His mother insisted that he and Junior and Phyllis Manning eat. Then, she said, he could bathe and go to bed while Junior took Nurse Manning back to pick up her car.

David lay down to sleep knowing that there were things he should be doing about his license. He was not sure what those things were. Anyway, he decided, they would be done later.

It seemed he had not slept at all when he was awakened by his mother. "Son, David." She was patting his shoulder. "Son Boy, listen."

He was still only half awake when he heard, "Some officers, they say they have to see you."

Many officers of all ranks had been at the crash scene. He supposed there was something they wanted to know, perhaps about identification. He put on a pair of trousers and slipped his feet into sandals, still not fully awake.

In the living room two uniformed officers were waiting. The older one asked, "Are you David Williams?"

When he answered the officer said, "We're from the sheriff's office. You are under arrest."

Suddenly he was fully awake. He heard "warrant

alleging practice of medicine without a license . . .
complaining witness Dr. Harold Boyd."

The second officer recited to him the memorized
statement regarding his rights. He had the right to
remain silent and say nothing, and anything he did say
could be used against him. He had the right to have a
lawyer, and if he could not afford to hire a lawyer the
state would provide one for him.

As he stood, scarcely believing, he saw through the
open door the sheriff's white car with its beacon
flashing red and white. They told him they would take
him to the county jail for booking. Bail might be
arranged after that.

"Please put your hands behind you." He complied,
and the younger officer quickly snapped handcuffs on
his wrists.

His mother screamed, "Oh, no! Don't do that! You
don't have to chain him up."

"The law . . . transportation of a prisoner."

His body was bending forward. His arms twisted
against the hard steel bracelets. "The law? The law?
To save lives and to go to jail for doing it? I say God
damn such a law."

Both the officers were standing back. Their hands
were on their guns. Mrs. Williams was voicing her
protest. She tried to hold to her son. Velvet was talking
low with sounds that were not words.

"Just settle down now, boy," the older officer said.

"We ain't trying to hurt you, but you give us a hard time and we going have to subdue you. You coming now?"

David knew what happened when an unarmed black prisoner tried to fight white officers who had guns. He checked his body movements and he nodded his head. "It's all right, Mamma," he said. "Don't worry about me, but you and Velvet, get ahold of Israel. Send him to the county jail. And call Dr. Hart. His number is in the small book by the telephone. Tell him what's happened. He'll know what to do."

He was put into the patrol car behind the heavy metal screen. It was awkward with his hands locked behind him. He leaned out and said, "Don't let Joyce Palmer come to the jail, only Israel."

With a blast of the siren the car turned down the drive and took to the road.

At the jail he was booked and put into a cell. There the handcuffs were removed by the jailer while one of the officers stood by with his hand on his gun. The cell had four bunks, but David Andrew Williams, M.D., was the only inmate. A bad smell hung in the air.

While he waited he reviewed his situation and decided it was not too bad—that is, if Mrs. McMillan did not develop complications.

"Oh, God," he prayed, "don't let her die."

He had friends, many friends. Israel would put up bail money. Dr. Hart would handle his defense. He well knew that in many cases doctors had rendered assistance in areas where they were not licensed to practice. Dr. Tennant at Methodist Hospital would be willing to testify that action was justified by the emergency. Dr. Kirkpatrick or someone else at Bellevue would swear that he was competent. There were others, the victims themselves.

His help came from an unexpected source. With a great clang of keys turning in hard locks, a door down the corridor was opened. Loud voices came into the cell.

"David, what the hell is this?"

It was John Campbell Boyd, "Little Red."

"They can't do this to you." A guard opened his cell door. "Come on. You going out of here. I signed bail for you."

David collected his personal possessions at the desk: wallet, keys, change. John Boyd, holding his arm, led him across the square to his office.

David told him what had happened, everything from the time he heard the crash through the treatment of the woman at the hospital.

"But why don't you have your license?" Red asked. "You've been here since the first of summer."

When David told him about the delays, the remarks at the office of the board in September, Red started walking the floor. "I know," he said, "that's Harold, and maybe his daddy's backing him up."

David had taken a seat near the window. He saw Israel's car with Velvet at the wheel. It braked to a fast stop. Israel jumped out and started running toward the jail.

From the door David called to Israel. Israel turned. He and Velvet hurried across the street to Red's office. Israel's arm went around David in a tight hug. Velvet was no less hearty in her greeting.

They were in haste to get him home—away from the jail, the courthouse, and all that they meant. David had to phone his mother before they left.

Red Boyd turned aside all offers of thanks. "I can't ever forget," he said, "that if it wasn't for David Williams I wouldn't be above ground today. I just can't see how my Cousin Harold can be so mangy-dog mean."

Twenty-Three

Velvet ignored the speed limits as she drove them back.

When David said he was all right, he had not been brutally treated, Israel disputed him. "The whole thing, the whole damn business, is brutal!" he said. "It's a brutal country when a man like Harold Boyd can have a man like you locked up, really for nothing."

He said it was the same as when Old Man Boyd had David's father locked up. While he was in jail Ed Williams had been beaten. He never fully recovered from that savagery.

"I swore that if they hurt you, David, I was going to get some of them," Israel said in his anger. "And I'm a God-fearing man, but I swear I ain't standing by to see no more of that stuff put on our people."

"Israel truly mean what he saying," Velvet added.

"And I'm backing him up. We Christians, but we ain't all that nonviolent."

These were his friends. David understood their feelings and he appreciated them.

"But the officers themselves," he said, "the two who arrested me and those at the jail—I believe they knew what they were doing because they acted like they were ashamed."

Velvet gave a grunt. "Ashamed, nothing," she said. "They was scared. You a right big man, you know."

They got to the house before dark. Joyce was there. She waited somewhat impatiently for Mrs. Williams to greet her son, then she put her arms around him and kissed him warmly—passionately—full in the mouth.

Junior was there. Nurse Manning had told him the whole story of the confrontation in the operating room. She had also described in detail the skill of Dr. Williams. Junior had repeated all this.

There were still more questions and answers and retellings of the events.

Israel boasted that everybody knew that Dr. David Williams was the one who had got everything together. Everybody, he said, would testify to that. David agreed that everyone out there, young and old, white and black, had cooperated. Each one had done what he could.

"It was beautiful," he said, "and it just goes to show what we can do right here in Pocahontas County."

Joyce agreed. "But there's another element," she said. "There's Harold Boyd as an individual. He is in there blocking and he will continue to obstruct, perhaps for a long time. But I don't think that is a matter of black and white. It's class. It's his class—rich, privileged, landowner. It's something almost feudal. And he's resisting the changes. He sees a poor boy, a peasant, never mind his color, but one of the peasants coming into the area and daring to challenge him. The whole thing is bigger than race, I say."

She could not convince the others. They saw the conflict as simply white and black. It had always been like that.

David had to explain again the injury and the surgical procedure. Junior cut in to say that the old white doctor had been afraid to tackle the job. Nurse Manning had told him that.

"I don't believe that any jury could find me guilty, even in the South," David said. "It was a real emergency, and as for the hospital, Dr. Von Schilling is chief surgeon and he insisted that I serve.

"When Harold Boyd shot off his mouth I tried to keep quiet, I really did, but I just couldn't listen to his lying to the patient about my qualifications. I couldn't take that."

"Well, David"—Velvet spoke bitterly—"you ought to know. He's young but he's got a lot of the old rebbish South in him, him and his daddy still wanting black folks to stay in their place, somewhere low and especially somewhere under the great white man."

"Yes," Israel added, "and that was a white woman you put your hands on. He couldn't take that."

"Not even to save her life," Mrs. Williams said.

Not even to save her life, they all agreed.

At six o'clock they were still going over the events of the day. Mrs. Williams called them to dinner, which she and Velvet had prepared. Nurse Pegram came reporting that all the injured people had been removed from the Saunders home. Ambulances had taken them to the V.A. hospital and to the Methodist Hospital, as well as to Boyd Memorial. When she learned of the arrest she joined in the angry protest, but she concluded with assurances that most doctors would support David.

"I've worked north and south," she said, "and I know doctors have less prejudice than most people. Their training and experience helps them. That Dr. Boyd, he's got a lot to learn."

Mrs. Williams said there was plenty of food for everyone. Without too much reluctance they settled down to eat.

Dr. Hart arrived. He had left the campus without stopping for his dinner.

"Maybe I'll just take a bite," he said, but he accepted a well-loaded plate of hot food and sat at a coffee table where David joined him. He listened to the full account of all that had happened, just listened without asking questions. Finally he said that he would be making some investigations.

"In the meantime," he said, "we must press to secure your license to practice. We will lay before the board overwhelming evidence of your competence and your character, and we will show the need for additional medical services in the area."

Nurse Pegram was saying her good-byes when another car drove up.

Dr. Tennant had come from Methodist Hospital in Capital City. He was in a cheerful frame of mind. He agreed to have a cup of coffee.

"We've been awfully busy too," he said, "and it was sort of like old times with Nurse Pegram taking care of the injured ones out in the field."

He went on to say that he had heard all good things about the doctor who led in the rescue work. "I can tell you, Dr. Williams," he concluded, "you came just at the right time and everybody was mighty glad you did."

David laughed. It wasn't funny but he laughed. Israel took it up. He gave vent to his amusement and his bitterness with loud guffaws. The others joined. It was a mild hysteria.

Dr. Tennant did not understand. He heard, "Everybody." "He says everybody." "Not everybody at all!"

When they quieted down, David explained that he

had been arrested for practicing medicine without a license.

"Arrested? No license?"

Dr. Tennant rose from his seat. He moved about almost as though he were in a daze. "But that was . . . before. . . . Surely you've gotten your certificate of license by now."

He explained that on the first day of October, when Dr. Williams told him that the license had not been received, he himself went to the office of the board. "I'm a member of the board, you know," he said. "I wanted to know what was happening there."

The executive secretary had shown Dr. Tennant the files. In response to the board's query, Dr. Boyd in South Town had indicated doubts regarding his hospital's use of the services of Dr. Williams. That was not legal reason to withhold the license, but the executive secretary felt a delay was justified.

"I told that young man what I thought and I got the chairman of the board on the phone. He backed me up. The whole thing was cleared before I left the office. Your license certificate was to be put in the mail that same day!"

"So Dr. Williams was actually licensed two days before the accident!" Dr. Hart was also standing as he spoke. "The allegations are of no effect whatsoever. I think we must sue that Dr. Boyd for false arrest."

"We just have to find why the papers were not mailed to you," Dr. Tennant said.

Junior had been listening but he had said nothing. Now he asked, "Did anybody check the mailbox today?"

No one knew. Junior turned and ran from the house. Excited remarks were in the air for the few minutes it took Junior to run to and from the mailbox on the post at the side of the road. He had several pieces of mail, including a long white envelope. "I bet that's it, Uncle David," he said.

It was.

It had indeed been issued on the first day of October.

With it was a letter of transmittal signed by the executive secretary. It closed with a paragraph which Dr. Williams read aloud:

The chairman of the board has asked me to say that he is pleased to know that you, having completed your studies in another state, will return to South Town.

EPILOGUE

My wife wanted to meet my friends in South Town.

The first of last June, with her beside me, I started driving down the New Jersey Turnpike. At Wilmington we crossed into Delaware and picked up Interstate Highway 95 to Washington. You can bypass Washington on the beltway, but I drove through the city just because I like the sight of the nation's capital.

South from Washington I picked up Interstate 95 again. We stopped in Richmond for the night.

The next afternoon I checked on the road map for South Town. Taking the proper exit, we reached the center of the town and turned south on Route One.

About four miles out we passed the Crawford place.

When we reached State Route 167, I turned right. About three miles west of Route One I saw the office of David Andrew Williams, M.D.

There it was. Four or five cars were parked outside.

I pulled off the road and stopped.

I turned off the switch and I sat there, just looking.

Ruth nudged me and said, "Come on. Aren't you going to take me in and introduce me?"

LORENZ GRAHAM

About the Author

Lorenz Graham was born in New Orleans, Louisiana. His father was a minister, and his childhood was spent in a succession of different parsonages. After graduation from high school in Seattle, Washington, the author attended the University of California in Los Angeles. In his third year, however, he left college to become a teacher at a mission school in Africa.

The great disparity between the American idea of Africa and the reality of African life first prompted Mr. Graham's interest in writing for young people. On his return to the United States, the author was graduated from Virginia Union University, and he later did graduate work at the New York School for Social Work and at New York University.

Lorenz Graham likes working directly with people and their problems. He has been a social worker and a probation officer. Most of his time is now given to his writing and to teaching in the English Department at the California State Polytechnic University.

While in Africa, Mr. Graham met his wife, who was also a teacher. They make their home in Claremont, California.